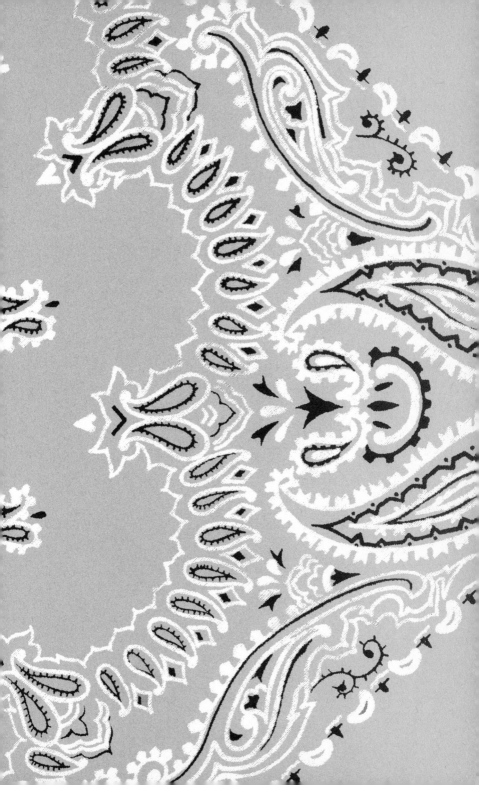

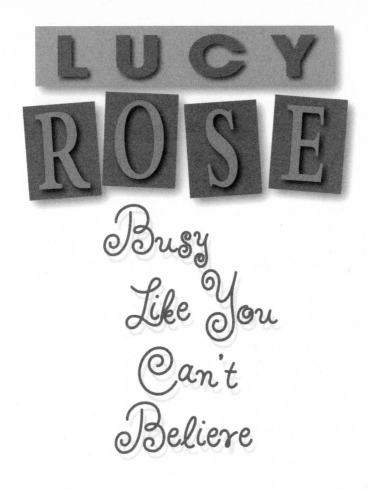

LUCY ROSE

Busy Like You Can't Believe

by Katy Kelly

ILLUSTRATED BY ADAM REX

Delacorte Press

Published by Delacorte Press
an imprint of Random House Children's Books
a division of Random House, Inc.
New York

www.randomhouse.com/kids

Educators and librarians, for a variety of teaching tools, visit us at
www.randomhouse.com/teachers

Library of Congress Cataloging in Publication Data
Kelly, Katy.
Lucy Rose : busy like you can't believe / by Katy Kelly ; illustrated by Adam Rex.
— 1st ed.
p. cm.
Summary: Now in fourth grade, palindrome-enthusiast Lucy Rose learns about the perils
of eavesdropping while also confiding in her diary her worries that her recently divorced
mother is beginning to date.
ISBN-13: 978-0-385-73319-9 (hardcover) — ISBN-13: 978-0-385-90338-7 (Gibraltar lib. bdg.)
ISBN-10: 0-385-73319-4 (hardcover) — ISBN-10: 0-385-90338-3 (Gibraltar lib. bdg.)
[1. Eavesdropping—Fiction. 2. Divorce—Fiction.
3. Family life—Washington (D.C.)—Fiction. 4. Washington (D.C.)—Fiction.
5. Schools—Fiction. 6. Diaries—Fiction.] I. Rex, Adam, ill. II. Title.
PZ7.K29637Lt 2005
[Fic]—dc22   2005023593

The text of this book is set in 14-point Goudy.

Printed in the United States of America

September 2006

10 9 8 7 6 5 4 3

First Edition

For Emily and Marguerite Bottorff,
adored daughters

You are fabulinity.

AUGUST

August 31

Here is what I am supposed to be doing: sleeping.

Here is what I am doing: standing on my bed on top of a tower that's made out of my folded-up pink dotty bedspread plus 4 pillows which is what I always do when I need to see my whole self in my rather teensy mirror and check if I look divine which, luckily, most of the time I do. Actually, that was what I was doing 2 minutes ago. But right when I was making positive sure that I was looking gorgeous in my tomorrow outfit, my tower collapsed every which way and I went flying and klonked my elbow and 1 cowgirl boot zwooped off my foot and crashed into my alarm clock and knocked it off my night table. That made a bouncing, clunking sound that made my mom holler up the stairs, "Lucy Rose Reilly! I REALLY hope your lights are OUT and your eyes are CLOSED."

I did not answer but I did think. What I thought was that since she was just HOPING and

1

not actually EXPECTING, I could stay up for a few or maybe 13 more minutes, if I was quiet in the extreme. Usually I'm not one for stretching rules but I seriously needed 1 minute to put on my Washington Nationals sleeping shirt, which I just did, plus 12 more because I have to write all my thoughts in this deluxe book that my grandfather, who's named Pop, gave me on account of I'm starting 4th grade tomorrow. That's also why I want to look divine because I am planning to make an impression on my new teacher who I don't know 1 thing about except for her name and it's Mrs. Timony.

Pop gives me a fresh book whenever I have an occasion. It's always red on the outside with lines on the inside. Pop says that when you are an original thinker, and I am original in the extreme, you should write about your life and I do because I have the kind of life that is mostly hilarious. This new red book has sequins on it. Melonhead, who is my friend that's a boy but NOT a boyfriend, called it "girly."

I said, "Of course it is. Sequins are the exact thing that they put on movie star dresses so they can sparkle when they walk."

Melonhead rolled his eyeballs at that.

Here's what I am wearing on the first day of 4th:

1. My red cowgirl boots that my dad gave me that were made in the country of Brazil but he bought in the city of Ann Arbor, Michigan, because that's where he lives.

2. A skirt that my Michigan grandma named Glamma sent me by Parcel Post. My mom says it's not the most appropriate for school on account of it's shiny pink and has a petticoat that makes it stick out, which is exactly the reason I love to wear it. Also because when I do twirls in that skirt, I feel confidence.

3. My orange T-shirt that's the same exact color as my hair.

4. My yellow bandana, of course.

If I had pierced ears like my absolutely greatest friend, Jonique McBee, I would look ultra-divine. Ultra means super and I learned it from my toothpaste tube and it's my Word of the Day. I'm collecting a vocabulary. Also palindromes, which are words that are the same backward as forward. Pop is one.

Now I am going to try to go to sleep but I

will not be surprised if I stay awake until 3:27 AM in the morning because thinking about 4th grade is making my nerves feel like they are jangling. My outfit is lying on my floor next to my bed looking like a flat person with no head. I did that for organization.

SEPTEMBER

September 1

This day started at the crack of 7:32 AM in the morning. Luckily, I am a speed dresser because at 7:38 AM there was knocking on the door and I had to slide down the banister for added quickness and when I opened it, there were Pop and Madam, who is my palindrome grandmother, and their maniac poodle named Gumbo, which is actually the name of a soup.

"We're here for the 1st Annual Back-to-School All-You-Can-Eat Family-Breakfast Extravaganza!" Pop said. He is one who loves an extravaganza. I am another one.

The other thing we go for is demonstrations. By the time my mom got downstairs Pop was doing egg juggling and singing a song to Madam called "Don't Go Bacon My Heart, You're Eggs-actly the Girl for Me." That song is homemade by him and it had us laughing our lips off but it made Gumbo leap around in a poodle panic and that made Pop drop an egg on his foot and it broke. The egg, not the foot. That egg caused Gumbo to think in his brain, which Pop says is not the biggest, "Free food!" So he started licking Pop's toes and leg and wouldn't stop until there was only shell left and Pop's leg was slimy with dog spit.

"Luckily raw eggs make dogs have shiny hair," Pop said.

"Maybe dog spit will make you have shiny leg hair," I said.

"That has been my lifelong dream," Pop said.

He might have been kidding.

Inside, Pop cooked pirate eggs while Madam cut up pineapple boats and my mom poured milk and I set the table. But then there was more knocking and more barking and my mom said, "It sounds like we'll need 2 more plates."

"Yippee-yi-yo, cowgirl!" I said. "I bet it's Jonique and Melonhead!"

"Adam," my grandmother said. She calls him Adam on account of that's his name.

Then my mom said, "That nickname has got to be bad for his self-esteem."

Those 2 ladies are in love with self-esteem.

"If Melonhead gets any more esteem he'll be the Number 1 know-it-all in America," I said.

Even though he's our friend, sometimes Melonhead acts like he's the only one in charge. Right away, one second after he came inside, he started rushing me like mad, saying, "Let's go-go-go, Lucy Rose!"

I think anybody would agree that is a bothersome attitude.

"We have time galore," I said.

"That's what I already told him," Jonique said. "It takes 2 minutes to walk 1 block, so it'll take 12 to get to school plus 2 more for red lights. If we go now, we'll be too early."

"Jonique, you're a mathematical genius," Pop said.

"I get it from my dad," Jonique said.

Her dad's an accountant at the government. I don't know what he counts but it must be something important because he's the boss of some people. Once, when Pop and I were in private, I told him that even if I got to be a boss, I wouldn't want to account. Pop said he himself is a word man, which I say is lucky since he writes stories for a job.

Melonhead stopped his rushing the second he

said, "I smell food," and plopped himself down in Pop's chair.

Even though Melonhead already had 2 bowls of Lucky Charms at home, he ate 3 hunks of coffee-cake and so much pineapple that there was none left for Madam and she had to eat a nectarine instead. He is not the most polite.

When the extravaganza was done my mom took pictures of us on our front porch with our new backpacks that are full of 4th grade supplies including ballpoint pens that are something you are not even allowed to touch in 3rd.

Pop said, "Lucy Rose, that is a fine outfit!"

"I know," I said. "I feel like a million dollars!"

"All green and wrinkly?" Melonhead said and started up with his hyena laugh.

I laughed too but Jonique looked huffy at him and said, "Lucy Rose's skirt is the best," so I'd feel like I was defended.

"I believe it cost 1 ton of money," I said.

"No doubt," Jonique said.

Then, while we were walking to school, Melonhead said, "Of all the dopey ways to spend perfectly good dollars."

"You would spend them on candy," Jonique said.

"I would spend some on candy," he said. "I'd spend the rest on baking soda and lime Kool-Aid and vinegar."

"Why on Earth?" I asked him.

"One day I'll show you," he said. "And you'll be amazed."

At school, Mrs. Timony was waiting for us by the 4th grade line-up that is on the complete other side of the school from Grades 3 and Under. She has red eyeglasses and a smiling mouth and wildish hair that I told her is a thing we have in common. Then I said, "I can already tell that this year is going to be plenty delightful!"

"Of course it is," she said. "I've been in 4th grade for 22 years and I always have a wonderful time." We got settled down in Room 7, which is a room I like because it has 5 windows and a fan that hangs down from the ceiling and spins, plus it smells like spray cleaner. Then Mrs. Timony said, "Let's start by shaking hands."

We had to stretch our arms because our desks are apart on account of we have more maturity than we did in 3rd when they were clumped into tables. On one of my sides is Clayton Briggs who is A-OK and on the other one is Ashley, who is P-U. I am sure about this because even though she is new at school and even though Mrs. Timony said we will all enjoy knowing her, Jonique and Melonhead and I have already been knowing her all summer and that experience has not been one speck pleasing to us. But Ashley said, "Hi, Lucy Rose," and gave my hand a big shake like she was feeling thrilled. That was a shock to me, but I was also glad because at least she was trying. I said, "Hi, Ashley!" and shook back. It was probably because of her excitement that it felt like she was crushing my finger bones.

Then we had to tell about ourselves. Mrs. Timony started and here's the thing about her: She has a husband and a son and her daughter plays the guitar at a nightclub plus she's in love with insects. She picked me to go next, which I say is an honor and Jonique agrees. I said: "This was my 1st entire summer of living in Washington, D.C., plus I play the cello and my teacher says I'm advanced for my age, which is 9. Also I know how to make some things. My mom's an artist that works at Channel 6.

My dad's a teacher in Michigan where I used to live but he comes to visit me."

That made a new kid blurt out, "I just moved here from London."

So Mrs. Timony asked her: "What have you found to be different about the United States, Hannah?"

"It's hotter here," Hannah said. "And in America you call chips French fries and you call crisps chips."

That is fascinating to me.

Hannah has brown hair that's short and her voice sounds like she's rich, which I'm pretty sure she is because her dad works at the embassy of England for somebody that's called Ambassador, and one time he met a real prince that was a kid, if you can believe it, which I do.

The second that she stopped talking, I waved my hand so fast that Melonhead said, "You look like a windshield wiper."

Mrs. Timony said, "Do you have a question, Lucy Rose?"

"I have a comment," I said.

"Yes?" Mrs. Timony said.

"Hannah is a palindrome," I said.

Hannah made a grin at me. She already knew that newsflash because it turns out when you have the name of Hannah, people are always telling you you're a palindrome. But none of the other kids had figured it out, which was pleasing to me.

When school let out, Jonique raced home and I kept going to my grandparents' house. Pop and my mom were waiting and drinking fizzy water on the side porch that has swinging baskets with purple petunias. Madam, who makes it her business to give people good advice, was taking a break from writing her newspaper column so she could hear my News of the Day, which she calls Scoop du Jour because she knows French from when she was a kid and lived in New Orleans, Louisiana.

"Robinson Gold has a pink stripe in her hair," I said. "A kid at her camp put Easter egg dye in it and the only way to get it out is to cut it but she's not going to because she loves it."

"That might be the Scoop du Summer," Pop said.

Then I told about Mrs. Timony and about Hannah from England. "At recess Melonhead called her Hannah-banana, which I do not think she loved," I said.

"I imagine if your name is Melon you get in the habit of calling people fruity names," Pop said and then Madam gave him a look like he's impossible.

"Here's another Scoop du Jour: Ashley was nice to me at handshaking," I said.

"That's an improvement," my mom said.

"That's a miracle," Pop said. "Now, how do you rate Day 1?"

"My rate is: great," I said. "But the thing I can't believe is in 4th you get homework on the 1st day."

Pop couldn't believe it either. He is against homework unless it's the creative kind and not from textbooks, either, because, according to him, they make kids' brains go dull. My mom did believe it. "You get to work and I will too," she said and she kissed the tip-top of my red head. "I'm on the overnight shift so you get to spend the night here and I'll be back in time for breakfast."

"The subway will be closed when you get off," Pop said. "Do you want to use our car?"

"No, thanks," my mom said. "I can catch a ride from a guy at work. He drives straight down Constitution Avenue, so he doesn't mind."

Then Madam looked at the Pop clock, which is what we call the grandfather clock, and said, "Oh no! I'm ON DEADLINE. My column is due in an hour! My editor is waiting and a lady from Bethesda needs to know what to do with a teenage vegetarian who won't eat any vegetables except potato chips."

Madam's column is in the newspaper and it tells parents what to do with their kids, especially if they have the kind that are disagreeable to others. The name of it is Dear Lucy Rose. That's because we have the same name only she has had it for longer. On Deadline means I can't interrupt unless I am bleeding.

"I'm On Deadline too," I told her. "I have to write a paragraph called 'My Summer Adventure.'"

But first, I wrote this e-mail on Pop's computer: "Dear Dad,

"Since Michigan teachers had to go back to school today even though the kids are still lolling about on vacation, I have 2 questions. 1. Did they have coffeecake in the teachers' lounge? 2. Do you know if anybody I know is one of your students?

"I love you a bushel and a peck."

September 2

At 6:22 AM this morning I got my cello, which I've been learning ever since I was 6, and for a treat, I tiptoed into Madam and Pop's room and played a wake-up concert. Pop said it was another sign of my original thinking because, he said, "an average thinker would just use the alarm clock but waking up to an unexpected cello recital is, in fact, much more alarming."

"Thank you," I said.

While they were getting up, I got my e-mail and it said:

"Dear Lucy Rose,

"Did I eat coffeecake on the 1st day of school? Did I? I did. Actually, I did not but 'Did I? I did' is such a swell palindrome I had to use it. Unfortunately, there has been a health uprising in the teachers' lounge so we had bagels and fruit. 2: Your cousin Drew is in my 7th grade homeroom. Aunt Betsy brought him and your 2 youngest cousins to visit my classroom and in the time it took me to give my sister a hug, Georgie crawled across the room and unplugged the aquarium and

Didi ate a piece of chalk. Aunt Betsy said, 'They'll be in Drew's seat someday.'

"I told her: 'I'm happy to teach all of your kids as long as they come 1 at a time because I don't know how you handle all 7 at once.'

"She said you get a minivan and you get used to it.

"I love you. You bet your pretty neck I do,

"Dad"

September 3

After school I told Pop that if Jonique and Melonhead and I didn't get cool drinks in 3 or less instants we'd perish from heat on that spot, which was the sidewalk. Perish means we'd absolutely die from it. Pop said he couldn't just stand there when simple limeade could save us, so he called for Madam and took us all to Jimmy T's restaurant.

After we got our ades Pop said, "Tell us who had the best summer adventure."

"Pierra Kempner moved and now she doesn't have to share a room with any sisters," Jonique said.

"That is the opposite of exciting," Melonhead said.

"Kathleen Sullivan went paddle boating on the Potomac River with her dad," I said. "They paddled right over to the Jefferson Memorial and waved at tourists and could practically touch the land of Virginia."

"Sensational," Pop said.

"Very sensational," I told him.

"Marisol Fernandez was too shy to read her homework so Mrs. Timony did it for her," Jonique said.

"Mrs. Timony did her homework for her?" Pop said. "Hot diggity-dog! That's my kind of teacher!"

That joke made Melonhead laugh so hard that limeade came out of his nose, which made Madam feel alarmed but I told her, "He is one boy who enjoys fizzing nostrils."

"How did Sam Alswang spend his summer?" Madam said.

"He got to take a jet plane to Atlanta, in Georgia, so he could visit his grandparents and they let him eat dessert 2 times a day," Melonhead said.

"What did you write about, Adam?" Madam asked.

"How I saved your apricots from disaster," he said.

"Mrs. Timony said she felt impressed with that," I said.

"I wrote about Parks & Rec and Vacation Bible School," Jonique said. "And going to my family reunion."

Then I said: "I told about my big adventure with my dad and doing my big project with my mom and about making a key chain out of Gimp. And that's when the miracle of yesterday was over because Ashley said, 'Some key chain,' in her stinky voice. And I think she would have been in trouble but she said it so low that Mrs. Timony didn't hear her."

"But I jumped up and said, 'It WAS some key chain! It was a GREAT key chain!'" Melonhead said.

"Mrs. Timony did hear that," Jonique said.

"And she said I should take a seat," Melonhead said.

"What did Ashley write about?" Pop asked us.

"Going to White Flint Mall with her dad," Jonique said. "He let her pick whatever she wanted and she picked 9 outfits plus sunglasses!"

"My goodness!" Madam said.

"Today she was wearing sky blue pants," I said. "And in my deepest heart, I wish they were mine."

"Sky blue pants don't make the girl," Pop said.

"These pants do," I said. "They are fabulinity."

"They are what?" Madam asked.

"It's for when something is fabulous until infinity," I said. "I made it up."

"Are my pants fabulinity?" Pop asked me.

"No," I said.

"Not at all," Jonique said.

"Well then, I share your despair," Pop said.

"Did you tell Ashley that you like her pants?" Madam asked. "I find it helps to share good thoughts."

"No," I said.

"Well, maybe she was also secretly wishing she had an outfit like yours," Madam said.

"Definitely not," Jonique said.

"She called my pink skirt CHILDISH," I said.

"Nonsense," Pop said. "It takes an original thinker to invent her own style. Lucy Rose, your look is unique."

"Unique?" I said.

"Unique means THE ONLY ONE," he said. "I feel certain there isn't another look like yours anywhere in the world."

Pop has a good talent for making a person feel better.

September 4

Today was the last day of the 1st week of school and so far, I like everything except Ashley.

Tomorrow my mom and I have to do nothing but work and run errands because we need new fruit and we have to buy pots of flowers called mums that are yellow. According to Hannah, MUM means MOM in the kind of English they speak in England. The odd thing to me is that they do not call a DAD a DUD, probably because it would make him feel bad. I'm going to start calling my mom Mum, so she can be my 1st palindrome from over seas. The palindrome, not my mom. She'll still be from America.

Since I'll be planting mums, I'll be too busy to go to Madam and Pop's. That is lucky because Pop is going to put a new flusher in the toilet and that is not a thing I want to watch. Melonhead can't wait. He is one who loves to see the guts of things.

"Even toilets?" I said.

"Especially toilets," he said.

When he asked if he could help, Pop said, "I'm counting on you to be my able assistant."

"I'll be the plumber's friend!" Melonhead said and cracked himself up. "Let's take that toilet apart right now."

"We'll start bright and early tomorrow," Pop said.

Melonhead went so wild with excitement that anybody would think he won the Olympics.

September 5

Jonique and I planted the mums that my mum kept calling the moms and I told her: "Sometimes you are hilarious." That was a pleasing thing to say because we are one family that loves hilarious.

Now our yard is almost as gorgeous as the McBees' even though we don't own one single lawn ornament.

After lunch Jonique and I got our scooters and scooted to Independence Avenue so our legs would get exercised. Then we had to lie down on the Presbyterian Church steps for a rest so we wouldn't feel utterly exhausted. Utter means the same as complete. That's when Melonhead ran up waving a red ball on a stick, yelling, "Look what I got!"

Jonique and I sat up and petted it. Then she held it up like a balloon and I asked, "What on earth is it?"

"It's the old float ball from inside the back of the toilet tank," he said. "Pop said I could keep it for a souvenir."

"P-U," Jonique said and threw it down and wiped her hands on her shirt.

"Disgusting," I said and I wiped my hands on Melonhead's shirt.

"It's only ever been where the clean water goes," he said.

"We don't touch toilet parts," I told him.

"Absolutely never," Jonique said.

Melonhead was way too thrilled to care.

Tonight my grandparents came over for a cook-out but Pop was too tired to play Scrabble. "I told Melonhead we'd start work bright and early," Pop said. "He arrived at 6."

My mom, I mean mum, had a laughing riot at that.

"Then an alarmed Mrs. Melon called at 7," Pop said. "Apparently, he forgot to tell her he was leaving the house."

"She's the kind that worries," I said. "And he's the kind that forgets."

"That keeps their lives interesting, then," Pop said.

"Does it ever," I said.

September 6

This morning, I typed this e-mail:

"Dear Dad,

"Who ate the chalk? DIDI DID.

"Love, your palindrome-inventing daughter"

Here is what I got from my dad:

"Dear Lucy Rose,

"You are a brainiac and I love you."

So I wrote:

"Dear Dad, I am a word person. And I love you back."

September 7

This was supposed to be a great day because it's the labor holiday, which I used to think was for ladies who had babies. It actually is for people who work, which kids do a lot so we get the day off from school.

But it turned out to be one very bad day and now I am having a bad feeling and it's in my stomach and my brain. Here's why: My mom and I were doing spelling quiz practice and the phone rang and I got it because usually it's my dad. But it wasn't. It was a man and he said: "Is Lily there?"

I knew right off it wasn't Pop, or Uncle Mike or Mr. McBee who only calls when it's time for Jonique to come home or Mr. Melon who just about never calls on account of he's working every minute at his job for a congressman. Luckily for me, Madam taught me telephone manners because according to her you can't get through this life without them. So, in my most delightful voice, I said, "May I ask who this is calling her?"

And he said, "This is Ned Eastman."

Who is one person I never heard of.

Unless he is that guy from work who drives her home because he doesn't mind.

Then my mom took the phone and said, "Lucy Rose, put on your pajamas and brush your teeth and we'll spell later."

Which made me feel like she wanted me to leave the room.

I did go but I stayed on the other side of the swinging kitchen door so I could hear but right away my mom poked her head out and said, "I'll be off by the time you are in your PJs."

Upstairs I got one of my sharp ideas and I picked up the phone in my mom's room. Then I heard Ned say, "Let's meet for coffee at 11 on Monday."

My mom said, "Sounds great."

Then she said, "Are you listening in, Lucy Rose?"

"No," I said and I hung up fast.

I ran into my room and changed in a snap and brushed my teeth in a half snap and ran downstairs and stood 1 inch in front of her so she would have to get off which she did.

"Do you want to talk about this?" my mom said.

She has a love of talking about things. Especially feelings. Especially when they are mine.

"I do not," I said.

"I do," my mom said. "Eavesdropping is bad manners. It is not okay to go upstairs and listen on my bedroom phone. If I catch you doing that again I will be very disappointed."

To me, disappointed is the worst punishment.

"Got it," I said.

"Good," she said. "Are you ready to spell?"

"Is Ned a date?" I asked her.

"Ned is a friend from work," she said.

"I would say you have enough friends," I told her.

"Lucy Rose, I know you know that Daddy and I will be officially divorced this month," she said. "Is that what you're worried about?"

"You can be divorced," I said. "But you CAN-NOT have a date."

"Honey, when people get divorced they usually go out with other people," she said, and she gave me a tight hug for a long time and then she said, "I hope that one day I will meet someone nice and I hope Daddy does too."

"You are making me feel like I'm horrified," I said.

And I left without spelling anything.

September 8

At recess, Jonique and I went to the little kid side of the playground for privacy so I could tell the terrible news. "A person named Ned called my mom.

And he's a man. And they are drinking coffee. I was listening in. My mom says he's her friend but I think he's a date. What if he wants to be her boyfriend? Or if he wants to marry her? If he marries her he will probably want to live with us. Then he'll think I'm his daughter, which I never, ever will be, no matter what he thinks in his Ned head," I said and I was almost crying.

"Are you sure it's a date?" she said.

"Pretty sure," I told her.

"Disgusting," she said.

"That is the same exact way I am feeling," I said. "Even though I don't want to think it about my mom."

"Your mom is NOT disgusting," Jonique said. "She is fabulinity. It's just that I'd hate to think of my parents on a date with somebody that wasn't one of them."

"I do hate it," I said.

"You should talk to Madam about it," Jonique said.

I felt thankful for that good idea.

September 8—
The same exact day but at night

Jonique's excellent-O plan was a flop.

After school Madam and Gumbo took me out for a smoothie, which seemed like it was lucky on account of I could tell about Ned. But before I did, Madam said, "Your mom told me you eavesdropped on her phone call. I was so surprised."

"How come?" I asked.

"Well, it's not respectful," Madam said.

"Does everybody agree with that or do some people think it's okay?" I asked her.

"Almost everybody agrees," she said. "But I have noticed that a lot of kids who are between 8 and 10 years old go through an eavesdropping phase."

"I am between those years exactly," I said. "I'm 9. I still have a year to go."

"No you don't," Madam said. "It's not respectful. Everyone is entitled to some privacy. Just think how annoyed you'd be if someone was eavesdropping on you and Jonique."

By then we were at the smoothie store. "I utterly

30

hope they have strawberry banana," I said to make a subject change.

September 10

Yippee-yi-yo, cowgirl! I am the luckiest duck on Capitol Hill. Here's why: Madam and Pop have to go hear jazzy piano playing at the Kennedy Center on account of it's their anniversary of getting married. And my mom got called to work the overnight shift because they are having a news emergency. So, even though it's a school night, Mrs. McBee invited me for dinner and a sleepover. That is one combo I adore like anything. McBee food is divine and it was tonight because we had BBQ and greens plus macaroni and cheese plus cherry pie with a la mode. A la mode is my Word of the Day. It comes from France and means with ice cream on top. I told the McBees, "I even like my ice cream with a la mode."

After we cleared the table, Jonique and I started dancing in the living room and when Aretha Franklin who is Mrs. McBee's dream diva started singing "R-E-S-P-E-C-T, Find Out What It Means to Me," Mr. and Mrs. McBee danced too and if you ask me they could win a contest on TV and get $100. When we were danced out, Mrs. McBee gave me a softy pink towel so I could have a shower in their ultra-deluxe bathroom, which is so gorgeous it could be in a hotel, plus they have soap that's called gel and makes you smell like a Peppermint Pattie. After I was clean, Jonique and I lazed about on the fuzzy yellow rug in her room that is a credit to Mrs. McBee and her excellent style because she's the one who picked out the flower wallpaper and pajama hooks that look like butterflies. Then Jonique asked me, "Did you find out more about the date?"

"Nope," I said. "Madam and my mom are against eavesdropping."

"Did they say, 'I forbid you?' " Jonique asked me.

"No. My mom said I can't listen in on her bedroom phone," I said.

"That's bad," Jonique said.

"But she didn't say anything about the kitchen phone or the one in the basement," I said.

"That's good," Jonique said. "What did Madam say?"

"That eavesdropping is not at all respectful," I told her.

"NOT RESPECTFUL is different than HAVE TO STOP," Jonique said.

"And she said how would I like it if somebody eavesdropped on us," I said.

"I wouldn't care so much," Jonique said.

"Me either," I told her. "Unless it was right now."

September 12

Pop and I were on a walk to Roland's Market to buy a *New York Times* because he has a devotion to doing cross words, and I asked him, "What do you think about eavesdropping?"

"I'm all for it," Pop said. "When I'm on the Metro, I try to sit near people who are talking, just so I can listen."

"Really?" I said.

"Sure. I hear all kinds of interesting things I never knew before. Last week I sat behind a lady who was cranky because her husband gave her a hedge clipper for her birthday."

"Now you know wives don't like hedge clippers," I said.

"I learned that many anniversaries ago," Pop said. "But I enjoyed hearing about this other husband. I find eavesdropping helps me learn how people think and what they talk about and that helps me be a better writer. Also, it's fun."

"This is information I have been needing to know," I said.

"You should try it," he said. "You're a natural writer."

"I'm a natural eavesdropper, too," I said. "Do you think it's fine if I practice on my mom?"

"No," Pop said. "I'm sure it would be fascinating but there are 3 Rules for Happy Family Living. 1. Do not open anyone else's mail. 2. Do not snoop in a lady's purse. And 3. Don't eavesdrop on the people you live with or their friends."

"I've never opened anybody's mail," I said.

Pop said he was proud about that.

September 14

The greatest thing happened and that is that the water main broke and made a huge flood in the street that made school get out at 11 o'clock AM. Since my mom was off, she picked me up.

"Where are we going?" I asked her.

"You'll see," she said. "Here's your Metro card."

"I like to call it the TUBE," I said.

"Okay," she said. "Here's your TUBE card."

"Hannah says that's what they call their subway in England," I said. "Tube's the 2nd word in my vocabulary collection that's from a foreign land. I decided it counts because it's different than the American kind of tubes that come with toothpaste inside."

"Jolly good," my mom said. I don't know why.

We got off at Gallery Place and went up the escalator and under the fanciest arch with golden designs and Chinese writing. I could not believe there is something this gorgeous in Washington and I had never heard of it before. Don't ask me how I knew the writing was Chinese, I just did. I was right too because my mom said, "What do you think of Chinatown?"

"I think it smells delicious in the extreme," I said.

"Me too," she said. "Let's get Dim Sum."

I had no idea what in this world Dim Sum was but we found it in a puny restaurant that had chopsticks and food on teacarts that they roll around

and you can pick what you want. The first cart had nothing but sweet-looking buns. "They have pork inside," the waiter said. "And they are good."

"Excellent-O," I said, so I would be polite.

I ate a bite and my mom said, "What's it like?"

"A little sweet," I said. "And a little porky."

My mom got Sticky Rice in Lotus Leaf that sounded P-U but wasn't. Then another waiter said, "Steamed Octopus Ball?"

I said, "NO, thank you," before my mom could say, "Yes, please." She is wild for new experiences and thinks I should have as many as she can find. I am one who agrees with that idea except when it's the experience of eating octopus.

I did say, "Yes, please," to fried cakes that looked like Chanukah latkes but weren't. It was the first time I heard of taro root and also the first time I ate it.

Dessert was between Mango Pudding and Sesame Rice Dumplings. We played rock, paper, scissors and pudding won. When we were stuffed up to our necks, a waiter came to our table and counted our plates. That's how they know how much Dim Sum customers have to pay. There are 3 sizes of plates.

The things on the littlest plates are the cheapest. After we paid, we walked around the town holding hands and wearing out our eyeballs looking at Chinese things. One store had cooked ducks hanging in the window with their feet still on. Another one had red cloth shoes with golden dragons on the toes that are made of embroidery. We bought those gorgeous shoes for Jonique's birthday present and we got Mrs. Timony a cage for keeping crickets so she'll have luck. My mom got a jar of Tiger Balm in case anybody in our family gets a neck ache.

Then my mom said, "It's almost rush hour. We'd better shake a leg if we want seats on the Metro."

I gave her the look of one eyebrow going up.

"I mean the TUBE," my mom said.

"Thank you, my mum," I said.

This is what I call a glory day.

September 15

Madam is fond of family walks on account of they get oxygen in our blood, which she says is good for our hearts and, according to my mom, also good for her thighs. I never knew that thighs need oxygen.

On our walk today my mom asked me, "Have things gotten better with Ashley?"

"Not so much," I said. "Mostly she ignores me and Jonique and Melonhead and tries to get everyone else to like her and not like us."

"That's annoying," she said.

"Maybe she'll be kinder when she feels more secure," Madam said because she is one who goes for the bright side of things.

"I doubt it," I said.

"Me too," Pop said. "I'm afraid Ashley will always be the bane of Lucy Rose's life."

"What's a bane?" I asked him.

Pop laughed. "It means she's a big pain in your—"

"Elbow," Madam said and I think she interrupted.

"She's my bane, all right," I said. "A bane in my butt."

My mom and Madam are not fans of that word but Pop and I could not stop laughing.

September 16

Good thing: Mrs. Timony calls her cricket cage a treasure.

Not a good thing: I got the idea of putting my ear on the kitchen door so I could hear Madam and my mom because I felt like I absolutely had to even though my whole family feels like I absolutely don't have to. But I leaned too hard and the door swung open and I tipped over and landed on my side and smashed my knee and my thumb plus my face turned red but that was from embarrassment.

My mom said, "Oh dear, are you okay?"

And Madam said, "Whenever your mom had a growth spurt, she'd bump into walls and trip over doorjambs until she got used to her new size."

"I've probably been on a spurt myself," I said.

And I rushed right out of that room.

September 17

When my dad called I told him about Jonique's dragon shoes and he told me that our dog named Ellie Mae that lives with him in Ann Arbor went to the Purr-fect Pet Parlor and he said, "When I went to get her, her hair was so short I didn't recognize her at first."

"I would hate to not recognize her," I said.

"It'll be grown out by the time you see her but I'll take a picture and e-mail it to you," he told me.

"Good idea," I said. "A person should know what her dog looks like."

"She won't be the only one in the picture that has had a haircut," he said. "Tell me what you think."

September 18

All I do with my entire life these days is practice. First I do cello, which is fun. Then multiplying, which is not. I am fine at the 1 tables because who isn't? And I'm snappy at 2s and 5s and 10s. I'm okay at the low 3s and 4s but when they get high my nerves jangle and I can't remember what anything equals.

Even though Pop is against memorizing, he makes an exception for times tables. He says they are a must-learn.

I say they are P-U.

September 19

Our weekend homework was the creative kind and it was to write a poem about a bug. Here is mine:

A lady praying mantis is not polite.

When she sees a man mantis she eats his head in one bite.

September 20

When I saw Ellie Mae's photo I was shocked to pieces and had to e-mail to my dad: "Ellie Mae looks like she's cute but when you said you got your hair cut, I never in this world thought you meant your mustache hairs. But I am interested because in my whole life I had never seen that space under your nose."

P.S.

This is not eavesdropping because I did it with my eyes, which I believe is called eyedropping. I read my mom's list called To Do and it said: Buy yogurt.

Return library books. Paint front door red. Call Ned. Pinch dead blooms off mums.

Here is what I did: Erase Ned.

September 21

Mrs. Timony is a fan of fashion. Today she wore a necklace made out of tiny pencils that can really write. Our reading aide named Mrs. Washburn is not one for style because she mostly wears smocks. Also, she is not one bit cheerful and she has the kind of lips that automatically pinch themselves into wrinkles. Plus her vocabulary words are so easy that anybody who is not an absolute newborn infant knows them already. Plus the stories she likes people to read are dull in the extreme and never funny, which is the exact opposite of what I like in a book. The only pleasing thing about her is that she likes my poem. In front of the whole class she said, "It's very unique."

"Thank you," I said, and to be a big help, I told her, "By the way, it's impossible to be VERY unique."

Mrs. Washburn looked at me and her lips got even pinchier and her eyes looked like they were curious, I think because she wanted me to explain. So I said, "VERY unique is like saying VERY ONE OF A KIND but either you ARE one of a kind or you ARE NOT one of kind and, according to my Pop, I am. That's because there is no one else like me in this world."

It sounded like she said, "I'm thankful for that."

"You're welcome," I said. "And don't you worry about getting unique wrong. Grown-ups do it all the time."

Hannah and Jonique came with me to my grand-parents' and Madam gave us apples that are organic for our health but I pulled her ear down and whispered, "Do we have scones?"

"Only on Christmas morning," Madam said. "Why?"

"For Hannah," I said. "That's what they eat for snack in England only they call it having tea."

"I have tea," Madam said.

She made us some that's named Decaffeinated Green and put it in her silver teapot on the dining room table with teacups that have violets painted on them and napkins and cinnamon sticks for stirring and lemon chunks plus sugar with a spoon that's shaped like a shell and cake on a plate that's precious because Mrs. Greenberg brought it to Madam from Israel.

When Madam left to go upstairs, I ran after her and hugged her middle and said, "You saved my day."

"I'm glad," she said. "Sometimes you save mine."

I did not know that before and when she said it, I felt joy.

After we drank our tea that only tastes good with 6 or more spoons of sugar in it, we put our cups in the kitchen sink. "You're lucky, Lucy Rose," Hannah said. "At my house we just have Chips Ahoy and tea in mugs."

September 23—The Worst Day

I am feeling panic plus anxiety plus my stomach is swirling and not in a good way. Here's why: I was lying on the window seat in the living room, reading the comics, when my mom and Madam went in the kitchen. I did not want to be disappointing but then I thought, "What if they are talking about the

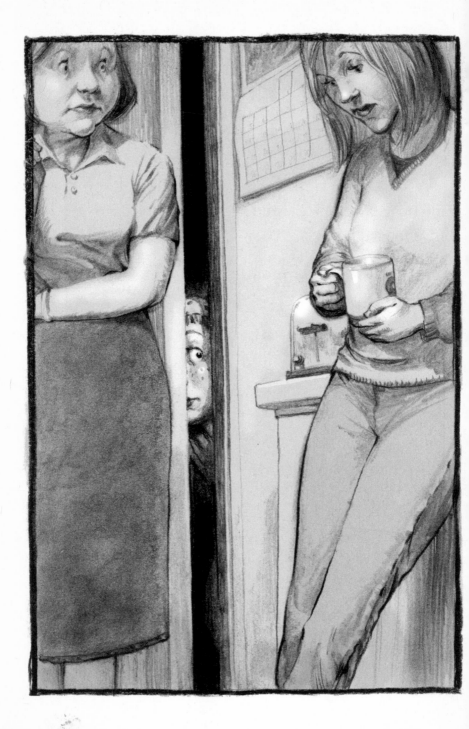

Ned that I dread?" That made me feel like I had to listen through the crack of the door. When I did I heard Madam say: "I saw Lola and Leon McBee walking out of the real estate office this morning. I hope they're not going to move."

"Oh! I hope not," my mom said. "But I know Lola misses her sister in North Carolina."

Then they were quiet like they were thinking to themselves until my mom said: "Lucy Rose would be devastated if they left Capitol Hill. Let's keep this a secret until we know for sure."

Devastated is a new word for me but I automatically know what it means: feeling like your heart is broken.

Now I am upstairs in my red room, scrunched under my pink bedspread, not telling what I heard on account of I don't want to confess about eavesdropping and wondering if Jonique knows she might be moving and feeling nothing but misery.

September 24

This morning was so roasting that I wore shorts to school and my mom wore her pink shift dress to work and I hope that Ned does not like pink. This afternoon, it was raining like dogs and my cowgirl boots got sogged. Luckily, Madam came to pick Jonique and me up in her purple station wagon. Melonhead wouldn't come because he wanted to get soaking with Sam. Madam said he should suit himself and took us home to eat soup that she made herself from a chicken.

"Do you think you'll ever move?" I asked Jonique.

"Never in my life except for when I go to college," she said.

I was quiet on account of I don't want her heart to feel devastation too.

September 25

We were lazing about on the lounging chairs on the McBees' back porch and eating Mrs. McBee's oatmeal cookies and talking about the greatest thing that happened today and Jonique said, "I want to be an orphan."

Then we heard gasping and there was Mrs. McBee, holding cups of pink lemonade and looking like she was feeling distress.

"Not in real life, Mama," Jonique told her.

"What other kind of life is there?" Mrs. McBee asked us.

"Stage life," I said. "We are having the musical of *Annie* at school and tryouts are in October. And I already know all the songs but I am going to practice singing 'Tomorrow' every single minute of every single day until then."

"What part do you want?" Mrs. McBee asked me.

"Annie, of course," I said.

"Of course," she said. "You're our Broadway baby."

"I'm no baby," I told her. "But I when I grow up I'm going to be a Broadway woman and be an actress for my job."

"Who else is trying out to be Annie?" she asked me.

"I don't think anybody is but even if somebody else does a tryout, I'm pretty much sure I'll get picked," I said.

"You are?" Mrs. McBee asked me.

"Yep," I said. "Because: 1. I am in love with musicals. 2. I have red hair like Annie. And 3. It's the desire of my life."

"I wouldn't like to be the one on the stage that everybody looks at," Jonique said.

"I do like to be that one exactly," I told her.

"I know," Jonique said. "You'll be even better than the Annie in the movie."

"And you'll be the greatest orphan," I said.

September 26

I have nothing but *Annie* on my brain so there's no room for other stuff. That's good because I don't want to think about the McBees moving but bad for multiplication memorizing. Yesterday, when I asked Melonhead how many tables he knew by heart, he said, "Most. But some of the 8s are hard."

"I would rather eat paste than do the 9s," I said.

"Who wouldn't?" he said. "I've eaten plenty of paste. I'd definitely pick paste over times tables."

"Paste is not an option," Mrs. Timony said. She can really creep up on a person in those softy shoes of hers.

"I can't keep the answers in my head," I told her.

"I'll tell you the secret," she said.

"Excellent-O," I said. "Tell me!"

"Practice, practice, practice," she said.

That's not the best secret, if you ask me.

"They are a bane to me," I told her.

"They are a bane to everybody until they learn them," she said. "After that, they're just a handy thing to know."

September 27

Today, when the phone rang, my mom answered upstairs, so I picked up in the kitchen and held my nose so they couldn't hear my breath but I could hear my mom say, "How are you?" in a friendly way that made me think it was Ned.

Instead, a lady said, "Dan's away on business, the washing machine is broken, the baby has a rash, and the school called because Harry spit on the playground, apparently on purpose and directly at someone, so I've had better days."

All this tragedy made my mom laugh her head off, which I thought was rude in the extreme.

"Molly," my mom said. "From one M.O.T.H. to another, how can I help?"

Then I figured out that Molly is Mrs. Mannix from the Moms on the Hill club.

"I'm off tomorrow," my mom said. "If nothing else, I could teach Harry to spit discreetly."

Mrs. Mannix started laughing and said, "Harry needs no help. He was born spitting. But could you pick him up from kindergarten tomorrow? I've got a doctor's appointment."

"I'm happy to do it," my mom said. "Are you taking Emma to the pediatrician for her rash?"

"No," Mrs. Mannix said. "I'm going for myself. I just found out I'm going to have another baby!"

"Congratulations!" my mom said. "That's wonderful!"

I kept right on listening until they started talking about Mr. Mannix's lawyer job because, let me tell you, that is one tedious topic. Tedious is my Word of the Day. It means tiresome, according to Madam, who thinks the most tedious thing is income taxes. Pop is right. Eavesdropping is a good way to learn the Scoop du Jour. Also new words. I figured out that discreetly means long distance. So spitting discreetly must mean my mom can spit a long distance. That's one talent I never knew she had.

September 28

Ashley brought a double-Dutch jump rope to recess and since she's the rope owner, she got to pick the jumpers and she picked Marisol and Kathleen and Jonique and not me.

"Lucy Rose is a great jumper and turner," Jonique said.

"That would be too many people," Ashley said.

Jonique's the champion of the sport of double-Dutch, so even though my feelings were hurting, I said, "You go ahead."

But Jonique said, "No thanks," and walked away.

She is my truest, blue-est, unique Jonique.

September 29

After school I practiced singing "Tomorrow" for 4 hours or more and I would have kept going but my mom said I should give it a rest. She is probably worrying that I will wear out my throat.

At recess I was practicing my eavesdropping on Mrs. Washburn who was telling Mrs. Timony that she was missing Mr. Washburn because he is visiting his married sister in Cleveland who can't hold on to her money. And, since I know about missing far away people, I gave her a recommendation. "Mrs. Washburn," I said, "you'll feel better if you talk to your husband discreetly."

She gave me a look that anyone would say was as odd as blue toast. I don't know why. I talk to my dad long distance all the time and it always makes me feel better.

OCTOBER

Ned called and I said, "My mom can't talk to you because she's in the bathroom," which was true but not
the thing to say because, according to Madam, when
you are the phone answerer you do not have to confide personal things like going to the bathroom.
Confide means telling somebody something.

"Would you leave a note saying Ned called?" he
asked.

"Okay," I said and I hung up.

I absolutely did not want to confide that message
but not leaving it would be a lie and I am no liar. What
I am is a problem solver. So I got out the teensiest Post-
it note and wrote in the puniest letters: Ned called. Then I
put it by the basement phone that we hardly ever use.

P.S. It turns out discreetly does NOT mean long
distance. It means not making a big deal so everybody
around knows what's going on, like when you want to
stare at someone but you can't because that is rude in
the extreme, so you pretend you're looking at the
whole, complete room and just rest your eyes on the
person for a second. That is discreetly.

October 2

After school Hannah and Jonique and I went to Madam and Pop's to do a fashion show which is one of Jonique's and my best things and we are always the models. Hannah found a dotty dress in the back of Madam's closet. I got a sparkle gown and Jonique tried on a blue skirt and a lacey jacket. When we did our display Madam told us she wore Hannah's dress to an election night party and she bought mine on a trip to Canada. "Where did you go when you were wearing Jonique's dress?" I asked her.

"Well," Madam said, "I wore it to your parents' wedding." I felt fascinated to hear that. Also a little sad.

After a while I told Jonique, "Why don't you wear this pink dress instead?"

October 3

Pop took me and Jonique to Jimmy T's for lunch and he got pastrami on rye bread and Jonique had a BLT and I was jumpy with excitement and I said, "Grilled cheese, please. Plus onion rings on

56

account of one thing I love is the smell of grease frying. And on top of that, guess what tomorrow is? Jonique's birthday!"

"Happy birthday, Jonique!" Mr. T said. "Ice cream's free if I can't guess your age."

He looked at her face from the front and from the sides and said, "This is too easy."

Jonique looked sad at that.

"You're 14," Mr. T said in his big voice.

Jonique practically fell off her spinning stool. "I am about to be 10 years old," she said.

"Free ice cream!" I hollered. "Mr. T, I cannot believe you thought Jonique was 14!"

"I always figured you 2 were the same age," he said.

"Lucy Rose is YOUNGER than me!" Jonique told him.

"No way," Mr. T said and even though he is the jokiest of all the Ts, this time, I could tell he was serious. When Jonique's ice cream came, all the Ts sang "Happy Birthday," which sounded like it was spectacular. So, as a reward for them, I sang "Tomorrow" and Mrs. T said she'll bring the T kids to see me when I'm Annie.

"Come early so you get seats in the front," I said.

Then, right when we were waving goodbye, somebody in the back called out, "Happy birthday, Jonique!"

It was Ashley's mom and sitting with her, eating hot dogs, were Ashley and Marisol.

"Thank you," Jonique said.

"We didn't see you in that far away booth," I said.

Then Ashley's mom, who has the name Rhonda, said, "You're trying out for the school play, Lucy Rose?"

"Yes, I am," I told her.

"Good for you," she said. Then she turned to Ashley and asked, "What about you, Doll? Are you going to try out?"

"No," Ashley said.

"Oh, you should," her mom said. "Tell her, Lucy Rose. Tell her the play will be a blast."

"The play will be a blast," I said in my plainest voice.

"It's for losers," Ashley said. "The only thing worse is playing the cello."

I think Ashley's mom was feeling embarrassed to have such a snippy daughter because she said, "Marisol, you want to be in the play, don't you?"

"Not if Ashley doesn't," Marisol said, but softly.

"And I don't," Ashley said, loudly.

"We'd better get going," Pop said. "My cello is waiting."

Then he made a wink at me.

On the way home Jonique said, "If I acted like that I would be in trouble from now until next month."

"Ditto," I said. That means: exact same for me.

October 4

After Jonique got home from church I gave her the dragon shoes so she could wear them to her party if she wanted to, which she did.

Then I could hardly wait for it to be 6 PM at night. At 4 PM, I put on my blue jean skirt and my wavey striped shirt with star buttons and I tied my bandana around my head like a bow and pinned a fake rose on it so I would look like I was festive and then I ate fish sticks because my mom said I had to and then it wasn't even 5 PM yet, so we played Go Fish and FINALLY it was time so we picked up Madam and Pop and walked to the McBees' and when we saw their dining room, I said, "I am dazzled and amazed."

That's because their house was even more gorgeous than at Christmas, which is usually its most beautified time. The table had pink cloth on it called satin and twinkle lights and there was a fountain and you could put your cup under it and catch as much red punch as you wanted. Plus after one look, I had to shout, "Dessert-o-Rama!"

Hannah shouted, "Smashing!"

"Don't you worry, Mrs. McBee," I said. "Hannah won't wreck your cakes. She's just speaking English."

Next to the fountain of punch, there was a lady that looked like Mrs. McBee, only shorter and with jazzier clothes, and Mr. McBee told us, "This is Lola's sister, Frankie. She came up from Durham, North Carolina, just for Jonique's party."

Everybody went crazy to meet Aunt Frankie. I liked her because she laughed at everything I said but I don't like that she's the reason Mrs. McBee wants to move. So I stood back by Melonhead, who was using his finger, which I am pretty sure was unwashed, to scoop yellow icing off Mrs. McBee's Zesty Lemon Cake and even though I told him to stop, he kept on doing it until he made a bald spot.

Then I said, "I think you don't have one single good manner in you."

"You're probably right," he said and wiped his fingers on the hang-down part of the pink cloth.

"Plus you're an absolute kook," I said.

"Great!" he said. "I've always wanted to be a palindrome."

I did not tell him that I had not figured that out until he said it.

Jonique blew out her candles with 1 breath and I knew she was wishing to be an orphan, which is the same exact thing I wish for her on my 2nd star of every night. I save my 1st stars for wishing Jonique will stay and Ned will leave.

Then Aunt Frankie said, "Sugar, tell me what you want."

I said, "Lemon cake and berry pie with a la mode, please."

Here's what Melonhead said: "A chocolate éclair, red velvet cake, 2 brownies, pie, 3 cookies, and mints, please."

"Is that all?" Mr. McBee said in his kidding voice.

"No," Melonhead said. "Just all that will fit on that plate."

At present time, Melonhead gave Jonique 3 grape ChapSticks, which is one of her best things to own plus they came in a little plastic purse that she can wear like a necklace. Madam and Pop gave colored pencils and a book like mine, only purple with no lines because it's for pictures, not words. Hannah's present was a jigsaw puzzle made of unicorns that came from the Fairy Godmother store. I know because I saw it in the window.

Then Aunt Frankie said, "Are you ready for mine?"

That present was as divine as anything because it's a fingernail kit that has 10 bottles of polish, 2 with sparkles, plus a nail file, plus lotion, plus a thing that's for putting between her toes when she's polishing, plus remover so she can take it off and start over. It all came in a suitcase to make it portable. That Word of the Day means she can take it where she wants and I hope she wants to take it to my house.

Mr. and Mrs. McBee gave her earrings that are made of genuine gold hearts. My mom's present went last. It's a picture frame that she painted herself with the same exact flowers that are on Jonique's wallpaper and it says Jonique & Lucy

Rose in cursive on top. In it is a photo of me and Jonique, wearing bathing suits, standing under the hose, looking like we will never finish laughing.

Jonique held that present on top of her heart.

October 5

I rate this day excellent-O. Our class took a bus to the Corcoran Gallery of Art and I was the luckiest because I got to sit in the front with Mrs. Timony on account of I get bus-sick.

We saw a show of quilts and here's what I think: People pay more attention when they are on walls instead of on beds. The other thing Jonique and I were adoring was the café. I ate noodles. Jonique got chicken fingers that came with free chips and we split a Sprite so we'd have $2 for the gift shop. Ashley's dad gave her $20 and she bought gum for all the girls except Jonique and me. I said I didn't care, but I actually did.

Tonight, I told my dad that I will take him to that museum the next time he comes to Washington.

"It's a date," he said.

"Good," I said. "But do NOT go on any real dates with any real ladies."

"What?" he asked me.

"You can only have the dates that are fruit," I said.

"What are you worried about, Lucy Rose?" he asked.

I did not want to tell about Ned so I switched the subject. "Have you ever had any students that are nice to some kids but try to make them go against other kids?" I said.

"Every teacher does," he said. "Some years I have 1 or 2. Sometimes I have a pile of them. Some kids have a hard time sharing friendships."

"How many do you have this year?" I asked.

"Just one," he said. "His name is Otis."

"Mine is Ashley," I said, even though he already knew.

I have to write 3 paragraphs called "Our Trip to the Art Museum."

October 6

Scoop du Jour: Mrs. McBee is making Jonique's and my Halloween costume because we're 2 people

64

going as 1 thing. When we told Mr. McBee what the thing was, he said, "Your idea is unsurpassed."

That means nobody in this world ever had a better one and I would say that is true.

I'm not writing our costume down in this book in case any eyedroppers try to peek but we did tell my mom because she borrowed Madam's station wagon and drove us to the Bruce Variety to get felt and ribbon and yarn. After that we drove to the Parkway Deli so we could drink chocolate malts with extra U-bet syrup.

This was a dream day.

October 7

After school I was helping Jonique unload the dish-washer because she always has to do that job before she can go outside and I heard Mrs. McBee wonder who would like leftover birthday cookies and Mr. McBee said: "How about Molly Mannix?"

"Not Molly," Mrs. McBee said. "I've noticed she's put on a few pounds lately and, believe me, no lady in that situation wants to be tempted."

"Tempt away, Mrs. McBee," I said. "Mrs. Mannix

isn't fat. She's just having another baby, and she thinks it's a boy and it's supposed to come on April 14th and she hopes it's not late because then she'll have to wear tents for clothes plus she can't wait until her husband's out-of-town trial gets over because between her busted washing machine and Emma's rash and Harry's spitting, she's worn out to pieces."

"You sure know a lot, Lucy Rose," Mrs. McBee said.

"Thank you," I said.

October 8

Before school I called my dad for a chat and I asked him, "How is Otis?"

"He threw Willa Isicoff's books out the window and had to spend the afternoon in the guidance counselor's office," my dad said. "How's Ashley?"

"Pillish," I said. "But she doesn't throw books."

"Well, that's something," my dad said.

October 9—
A Giant Red Alert Newsflash!

Pop and I were at the Trover Shop, buying a book to cheer up Madam's spirits because her sinuses were giving her a headache, and there was Mr. McBee, talking to Steve the owner, and Mr. McBee said, "Lola and Frankie found the perfect property. Now I'm trying to figure out if we can afford it."

On the walk home I asked Pop, "Would it be rude to ask Mr. McBee what he can't afford?"

Pop thought it would be.

By the way, I do not call that eavesdropping because Mr. McBee said it in front of the public.

October 10

Jonique and Melonhead and I lazed about all morning in Madam and Pop's far backyard and then we had a race up the back staircase and slid down the front banister on waxed paper to make it faster. When we got bored with that, we went to the

Melons' house that is so clean that kids are not allowed to go in the living room unless it's a special occasion so we sat in the kitchen and ate pimento cheese sandwiches while Mrs. Melon asked questions about the bruise on Melonhead's arm.

"How did that happen, darling?" she asked him.

"Beats me!" he said.

Mrs. Melon's voice got squeaky. "Who beats you?"

"No one beats me, Mom," Melonhead said. "It's just a bruise. I don't know how I got it."

"Maybe when you fell off the top of the jungle gym," I said.

"Or last week, when you were climbing on the breezeway roof at Madam and Pop's," Jonique said.

"How about when Sam boosted you up to look in the principal's window and your shirt got caught on the wire that keeps basketballs from crashing through and your wiggling made Sam fall and you were hanging by your sleeve until it tore and you fell and smooshed Sam?" I said.

That was when I got the idea we should stop helping him remember because Mrs. Melon was looking like she had anxiety in the extreme and she said, "Adam, if you promise to stay on the ground for the rest of the afternoon, I'll give you $1."

"It's a deal, Lucille," he said, even though her name is Mrs. Betty Melon.

"Don't you worry, Mrs. Melon," I told her. "We'll make sure he stays in low places."

On the walk to spend his dollar I told Melonhead, "You are so lucky. My mom never does bribes."

We bought Black Jack gum at Grubb's and chewed it up and stuck it on some of our teeth so it looked like they fell out. Then we walked around the neighborhood smiling and talking to people and we were a huge hit but by the time we got back Mrs. Melon had heard and was going frantic waiting to drive Melonhead to the emergency dentist.

October 11

Jonique came over and I acted like Annie and she acted like an orphan and I said, "You should drag your leg so people will feel pity."

She practiced dragging while we ate quesadillas and watched *Annie*, the movie. When it was done we sang all the songs, even the ones that star other people, to the phone so my dad could hear. He said we were perfection itself. When Pop and Gumbo came over to bring my mom a drill so she could put up coat hooks, I said, "Lady and gentleman, relax yourself on the window seat and get ready to feel like you're thrilled."

"I'm always up for a thrill," Pop said.

I sang all the *Annie* songs that are called solos by myself and then Jonique and I sang together and they both clapped like mad and my grandfather said he had no idea that *Annie* had so many songs in it. I was ready to sing another encore when Pop got the idea that we could do a song for Eddie at Grubb's. We did and I could tell from his look that he completely enjoyed it. "Would you like to hear another one?" I asked him.

He said he would LOVE to hear more but he had pills to count.

October 12—Right after school

Jonique and I ran zippy fast to Madam and Pop's. We found them drinking Red Zinger tea in the patio and I hollered, "Get ready for the greatest Scoop du Jour of all time!"

"Tell us," Madam said.

"Mrs. Timony made a big display on the bulletin board in the main hall and at the top she put up big letters that spell out OUR VISIT TO THE ART MUSEUM!" Jonique said.

"And she stapled up our papers," I said. "Plus pictures of us at the museum and fabric pieces and quilt posters."

"And since Ms. Boxley's 5th graders are making a quilt in art, she brought them all over to see our board," Jonique said.

"That's flattering," Pop said.

"But here's the thing about that bulletin board," I said. "Our whole class and their whole class were standing in front of it and listening to Ms. Boxley talk about patterns and then everybody started laughing and I had to hold on to my ribs. You know why? Because somebody had made a big letter F and put it up so it said OUR VISIT TO THE FART MUSEUM!"

"The 1st thing Mrs. Timony said was 'Where is Adam Melon?' " Jonique said.

"Now Melonhead has to stay after school for 2 afternoons and help Mrs. Timony clean out the supply cabinet," I said. "Plus they called Mrs.

Melon and she said she could shrivel up over the whole thing. But now the 4th and 5th graders think Melonhead is their hero, especially the boys."

Even though Madam doesn't go for that word, she and Pop laughed their heads right off. Then Madam said, "Teachers should be paid more than movie stars."

The exact same day but at 8:37 PM at night

Here is what I despise: multiplication. Despise is when you don't like something so much that you would say you hate it if you were allowed to which I am not because my mom thinks it is NOT POSITIVE even though I AM positive that I hate times tables. I'm even more despising since my mom got flash cards. Doing them makes me feel like my head is going groggy.

I'm getting better at the 7s and 8s, which are 2 of the worst, next to the 9s, which is the worst table of all.

Today Mrs. Timony had on a red bandana and I felt like we were twins even though mine is yellow, and the first thing she said was: "Attention everybody. Tryouts for *Annie* are in 13 days. I'm going to be the piano player and Mr. Welsh is the director."

"Mr. Welsh was my last year teacher!" I called out.

"And Mrs. Cunningham is going to be the choreographer," Mrs. Timony said.

"What's that?" Clayton asked.

"The dancing teacher," Mrs. Timony said. "There is a lot of dancing in *Annie*."

"Mrs. Cunningham has rhythm galore," I said.

"The play is open to all grades but I am hoping to see all my 4th graders at tryouts," Mrs. Timony said. "There are lots of good parts, starting with Little Orphan Annie."

I felt like she looked right at me when she said that. Then she told about Sandy the Dog and Miss Hannigan who is the screechy lady that yells at the orphans and tries to get money from Daddy Warbucks who is rich and bald.

That made Melonhead wave his hands until

Mrs. Timony, who is patient in the extreme, stopped her talk and said, "Yes, Adam?"

He said, "Does the person who is Daddy Warbucks really get all their hair shaved off?"

"Heavens, no!" Mrs. Timony said. "Don't worry. That actor will wear a bald wig."

"Oh," Melonhead said.

"Are you going to try out for that role?" she asked.

"Not if they make me keep my hair," he said.

October 14

I am being tortured by the 9 times tables. Today Mrs. Timony made a pop quiz, which is one thing I think should never be popped. Afterward Ashley looked at my pop quiz without any permission at all and said: "Did you get ANY right?

Later, when we were outside for P.E., Jonique told me, "Ignore Ashley. She has a bad attitude."

"A terrible, miserable, tedious, utterly P-U attitude," I said. "I wish I knew how to make her shape up."

"Has your dad been teaching for a long time?" she asked.

"Very long," I told her. "He said that every June he feels like he's been teaching for a thousand years."

"Of all the students he's ever had, how many have been problem kids like her?" Jonique asked.

"About a million," I told her. "I'd say my dad has AT LEAST a million. Probably more. He is loaded . . ."

I was going to say "with problem kids" and tell about Otis but right then I heard dirt kicking behind us and it was Ashley. I don't know how long she was there but I'm afraid she heard us talking about her. Jonique doesn't think she did because she says Ashley is the type who would yell her head off and tell Mrs. Timony so she'd get sympathy and we'd get in trouble. I would say she is that type exactly.

October 15

Tonight I called Pop on the phone and asked him if it ever snows in Washington in October.

"Almost never," he said. "Why?"

"I'm wishing for a snow day," I told him.

"That would put off the 9 times test," he said

because he knows my thinking. "But the *Post* says sunshine tomorrow."

"Are newspapers wrong sometimes?" I asked him.

"Sure," Pop said. "But usually not about weather."

"I am out of hope," I told him.

"I'm not worried," Pop said. "You'll learn the 9 tables."

"Not by tomorrow," I said.

"Probably not, but we'll love you anyway," he said.

"Well, at least I've got charm," I said.

October 16—The greatest day

Here is a miracle: Thanks to my most excellent friend, Jonique McBee, I am done with despising the 9 times tables. Here is why: At 7:30 AM, when I was brushing my teeth, Jonique hollered through the mail slot, "Open up, Lucy Rose! The answers are at your fingertips!"

I slid down the banister and opened that door and there she was with a Sharpie marker in one hand and her portable nail kit in the other one. "Put your hands on the kitchen table," she said.

"I am feeling despair galore," I said.

"Keep still," she said and she wrote a 1 on my left hand pinky fingernail and a 2 on the next fingernail and she kept going until she got to 10, which was on the pinky nail on my right hand.

"I know how many fingers I have," I said.

"Of course," Jonique said. "I marked them so everything is extra clear. Now pick a 9 times problem." I picked 9 × 4 because I already knew that one.

"Okay," she said. "Since it's 9 times FOUR take finger number 4 and tuck it under your hand."

"I don't get it," I said but I did it anyway.

"Look at your hands," Jonique said. "How many fingers are on the left side of your folded down finger?"

"Three," I said.

"Now count how many are on the other side of your folded down finger."

"Six," I said.

"Exactly. Three. Six. 36. 9 × 4 = 36," she said.

"Holy Moly," I said.

"Try 9 × 8," she said. "Fold down finger number 8 and see how many are left on the left side."

"Seven," I told her. "And 2 on the other side."

"Right," she said. "Seven. Two. 72. 9 × 8 = 72."

"I can't believe it!" I said. "Ask me another one."

She said 9 × 5 and I said 45 and kept going and got them all. "I don't need the numbers anymore," I said.

"My nail polish remover will clean them off," she said.

When my mom came down I was dancing around so fast that my cowgirl boots were clicking on the kitchen floor. "Ask me any of the 9 times," I said.

"Try 9 × 9," my mom said.

I folded down my number 9 right hand ring finger. "8 on the left, 1 on the right. 81. 9 × 9 = 81," I said.

"Oh, happy day!" my mom sang in her loudest voice.

I hugged Jonique until it sounded like she couldn't breathe. "You saved me!" I said. "Thank you."

"Actually, my dad saved you," she said. "When I told him your problem he told me that shortcut."

"That must be something they teach them at accounting college," I said.

"No doubt," she agreed.

At school I showed Mrs. Timony Jonique's 9 times finger trick and she let us teach it to the class and everyone got 100 percent, A + on the test, even Ashley.

October 17

Mrs. McBee brought us a coconut cake that smelled so delicious and nutritious that we all ate a piece even though it made our appetites too full for dinner.

"I am coconutty for this cake," I told everybody.

Mrs. McBee laughed at that.

"I'm not joking," I said. "You are a baking diva!"

My mom said, "Yum. It's made with real butter."

"I can't abide margarine," Mrs. McBee said.

Can't abide means she can't stand it one bit.

"Did you put coconut milk in it?" Madam asked.

"Yes," Mrs. McBee said, like she was feeling thrilled.

"It's a magnificent addition," Pop told her and to compliment her some more, he ate another gigantic hunk.

"I can abide another piece too," I said.

"No you can't," my mom said.

October 18

I asked Mrs. McBee: "Do you miss living near your sister?"

"Every day of my life," she said.

That was not the answer I wanted to hear.

October 19

This morning I made a sign that says: Come 1! Come All! See *Annie* starring Lucy Rose Reilly!

"You'd be a wonderful Annie," my mom said. "But no one can know who will be cast until after tryouts."

"I feel confidence," I said. "Plus no one in my class wants to be Annie."

"Don't take your sign to school," my mom said.

"Don't you worry," I said. "It won't get ruined."

"I'm worried that feelings will get hurt," she said.

"I'm only going to show Jonique," I said.

At school I waited until I had privacy with Jonique and also Hannah on account of she is a friend. Hannah called it brilliant, which is English for great, and Jonique said, "It's a beauty!"

Just then I saw Marisol and she saw my sign, which gave me the feeling that I was embarrassed like you can't believe. Later, I saw her talking to Ashley and I think it was about me.

When my mom picked me up I said, "I wish I took your recommendation."

"Some lessons a girl has to learn for herself," she said.

"Well, I did," I said.

October 20

Mrs. McBee is a goddess. Here's proof: She let me and Jonique help turn their front yard into a cemetery. For Halloween, not forever. Mrs. McBee had the job of cutting gravestones out of huge pieces of Styrofoam with her electric turkey-cutting knife. Jonique and I painted them gray with white splatters and green splotches that are the exact color of mold. Then Mrs. McBee glued on fake ivy and painted on names so it looks like they're carved in rock. One says: B. A. Frade. And there's Barry D. Bone. Miss Bea Haven is the littlest and I. M. Hansom is the biggest. The skinniest one says

Justin Tyme. "I don't know how you think up these things," Jonique told her mom.

"She's a word lady, that's how," I said.

Later when Pop and Melonhead came to see it, Melonhead said, "You should make one for Mr. I. P. Daley."

"That will not be happening," Mrs. McBee said. She liked Pop's comment better.

"Just to be able to walk by and look at the McBees' yard is a gift to the entire neighborhood," he said.

October 21

A very UNpleasing Scoop du Jour: Ned called. Since I was standing next to my mom in the kitchen, helping her wash beans, I could not listen in on the basement phone. But I was sorry to hear that whatever Ned said, it made my mom laugh.

October 22

Since the weather was absolutely nothing but sunshine and breeziness, I did my cello practice on the upstairs porch so I could look out and see 5th Street at the exact same time I was playing, "This Is the Song that Never Ends." And every time Pop and Gumbo walked by, Pop would yell, "Hello, cello!"

And I would holler back, "Cello yourself."

Then I would crack up laughing.

I made this e-mail for my dad.

"Dear Dad,

"THIS IS A TRUE EMERGENCY! Please ask Glamma and Shiralee and the other ladies that work at the Beauty Spot if they know a way to make my curly hair even curlier. Not for permanent, just for tryouts.

"Love,

"Lucy Rose"

I got a box from Overnight Express and inside was a hot pink bottle with a squirting top and a note that said:

"Dear Lucy Rose,

"This is Professional Strength Curl Enhancer. Rub it into wet hair. Do not brush. Let air-dry. Good luck!

"Love, Glamma & Shiralee"

October 26—Tryouts!!!!

My hair is looking very enhanced with so many curls that you would think I was the real Annie. Sometimes I do think it.

It took hours for it to get to be 3 o'clock PM but finally it did and we rushed to the auditorium for try-outs. I sat by Jonique and also Melonhead and Sam, who were trying out to be dogcatchers, and we listened to Mr. Welsh say the rules about always coming to rehearsal and that every part is important and about not talking while the director is giving directions, which I never would. Then he said: "Everyone interested in trying out to be an orphan, come to the front."

"That means you," I told Jonique.

"I'm scared out of my mind," she said.

"Don't be," I told her. "Just breathe and look at me straight in the eyeballs and sing from your heart."

"I think I'm not breathing," she said.

"You are," I said. "Remember to drag your leg."

Hannah and Pierra and Harry, the spitter, and about 22 other kids went up too. Jonique was number 6. Mrs. Timony asked which song she wanted and Jonique said, "Hard-Knock Life," and her voice started off nervous but then she looked at me and sang and was nothing but fabulinity.

Mr. Welsh said, "Jonique, that was inspiring."

But Mrs. Cunningham said, "I've got a concern."

"What is it?" Mr. Welsh asked her.

"This is a dancing show," Mrs. Cunningham said. "Jonique, do you think your leg will be up to it?"

"My leg is up to it right now," Jonique said. "I'm just faking."

"Why would you do that?" Mrs. Cunningham asked.

"I thought it would make me look pitiful," she said, which showed true friendship because she didn't say it was my idea.

When the orphans were done Mr. Welsh wrote some notes and then he said girls who wanted to get a lead role should come up. I sat in the very front chair so Mr. Welsh could have a view of me but he said, "Let's start with Ashley."

I practically fell off of my folding chair. I hadn't even seen Ashley in the auditorium and there she was onstage, wearing a curly red wig, singing "Tomorrow" so loud it felt like pins were poking my head. When she got done she made a curtsey and said, "Thank you," like she was the best person in America.

Then she sat by me, which got on every nerve I had left.

"You said the play was for losers," I whispered.

"Did I?" she said and got up and walked away and I do not believe that was a sincere question at all.

Right then, when I was feeling completely like I had no control, Mr. Welsh said, "Next up: Lucy Rose Reilly."

My cowgirl boots stomped up the steps and across the stage and my brain felt like it was frozen stiff and my stomach was in a ball and so were my hands and Mrs. Timony said, "What are you singing, Lucy Rose?"

" 'Tomorrow,' " I said.

Mrs. Timony started playing and I started singing but I was so furiously mad that my legs were clomping instead of walking and my words were coming out squealy and I could see Ashley laughing and I felt like running off the stage. Then I looked down and

there was Jonique standing up front looking right in my eyeballs. I looked back in hers and calmed myself and sang, " 'Tomorrow, tomorrow, you're only a day away,' " and it came out like I practiced.

Next a 5th grader named Dot tried out. She is a pleasing person but not the best at singing, which was a relief to me.

October 27

This morning, I made Melonhead and Jonique leave for school ultra-early so we could be 1st to see the Cast List but when we got there, no doors were opened so Melonhead ran off to balance on the top edge of the monkey bars before any teachers could see and tell him to get off because of it being against school rules, not to mention he could break his neck. That's a mistake teachers make. The thing about Melonhead is that if something's neck-breaking he wants to do it even more.

"Are you nervous?" Jonique asked me.

"More excited. I already feel like I'm Annie," I said.

"I'm afraid I won't get to be an orphan," she said.

"You will," I told her. "I hope you are one that gets to swing a bucket during 'It's the Hard-Knock Life.'"

"Or dance with a mop," Jonique said. "It would be fun to be a dancing, mopping orphan."

Then we stopped talking on account of Ashley was coming right at us.

"Are you waiting to see the Cast List?" she asked us.

"Yes," I said.

Then, after all the kid actors from all the grades were in a clump around us, Ashley said in her biggest voice: "Lucy Rose, do you REALLY think you'll get to be Annie?"

"I do think it," I said. But not in my biggest voice.

Just then Mr. Welsh came out and made a speech about everybody being a good actor and how it was hard to choose and how we should all congratulate each other. Then we all zipped inside and ran about 36 miles an hour, only Ashley pushed and got in front. By the time I got there she had a snarky look. I figured she was wild with anger about not being Annie so I made a friendly smile to show that I have sympathy for that.

Then I looked at the list. Right at the top it said: Annie. And next to Annie it said: Ashley. I started crying so hard it felt like I couldn't stop, plus my hands were shaking from grief and all I felt was embarrassed to miserable pieces. Then Ashley hollered, "Hey, Lucy Rose! Why don't you make some MORE Annie posters? Only this time, starring ME."

"Let's go," Jonique said and pulled me by my arms.

We sat on the library bench and Mrs. Ochmanek gave me tissues and water and Jonique told me, "You were the best."

"I feel the worst," I told her.

"Don't feel bad," she said. "I'm not on the orphan list."

For the whole morning I could not pay one speck of attention until Mrs. Timony said I should stay in for recess.

That's when she said: "You look awfully sad."

"I am," I said. "Awfully."

"You wanted to be Annie?" Mrs. Timony said.

"Like you can't believe," I told her.

"I can believe," she said and hugged my shoulders. "But are you at all happy with the way things turned out?"

Which made me think she had lost her brains. "No," I said. "Not the puniest bit."

"Lucy Rose, did you read the whole Cast List or did you just run off when you saw you weren't Annie?" she asked.

"I ran off," I said.

"Come with me," she said.

Jonique was sitting under some Hispanic Heroes on the hall bulletin board and Mrs. Timony said she could walk with us and when we got to the Cast List she told me: "Look again."

I saw: Miss Hannigan. Next to that name was: Lucy Rose.

"I have to be the mean lady?" I asked her.

"It's a terrific role," Miss Timony said.

I was about to say, "I am 1 person disagreeing with that," but I stopped because Jonique was jumping so high her braids were flying and she was yelling, "I'm Sandy, the adorable dog!"

It turned out that was her biggest dream, even bigger than being an orphan, only she was too shy to say it.

I gave her the biggest cheer, which was mature in the extreme because even when it's your best friend, it is hard to feel joy when you are stuck being Miss Hannigan.

October 28

My mom made French toast for breakfast even though we never have it on school days because it takes time, which we don't have on account of we are not morning people.

"Did you tell Daddy your big news?" she asked me.

"My big disaster, you mean," I said. "I did not tell."

"It's not a disaster," she said. "It's an honor. Miss Hannigan is a lead role. That's an important job."

"I'd rather be a lowly orphan," I said.

"Lowly?" my mom said.

"The lowliest of all the orphans," I said. "It's my Word of Yesterday. It means poor and pitiful and at the bottom."

"How can I help?" my mom asked me.

"You can homeschool me," I said.

"Ha!" she said, even though it was no joke.

At real school, I went straight to Mr. Welsh's room. "Hello," I said and I think my eyes were depressing to see.

"How are you feeling?" Mr. Welsh asked me.

"Lowly," I said. "I thought I'd be Annie. I practiced."

"I know," he said. "But we need you to be Miss Hannigan. She's a hard part to play."

"She's a bad part to play," I said. "So I'm quitting."

"Lucy Rose, last year you told me you want to be an actress on Broadway," he said.

"I am going to be one," I said. "In New York City, Manhattan, New York."

"Well, the Number 1 rule on Broadway is THE SHOW MUST GO ON," he said. "That means you're part of a team. Actors depend on each other and work together. It would be unprofessional to drop out just because you didn't get the part you wanted."

That made me feel a little bad. "But in real life I am the nice one and Ashley is the mean one," I said.

"You were the new kid last year," Mr. Welsh said. "Remember how it felt?"

"Yes," I said. "But I was not a crank."

I think he was ignoring that comment because the next thing he said was "I'll bet my eyeteeth that by opening night you'll be glad to be Miss Hannigan."

I turns out that eyeteeth are the ones 2 teeth over from the front teeth. They are also not something I want to own. Except the ones I already have, of course.

"I'll go to rehearsal," I said, but not in the friendliest voice.

October 29

My dad knew about my disaster because my mom told, so then he called me and said, "I love Miss Hannigan."

"I don't," I said.

"You'll shine onstage," he said.

"Doubt it," I said.

"I'm so sure you will that I'm coming to the show," he said.

"You're coming to Washington?" I asked him.

"I'll be the guy in the front, clapping every time you speak or sing or dance," he said. "And since Thanksgiving is that week, I'll also be the guy who wants a 3rd helping of stuffing."

"Hang on," I said. "I have to tell Mom this Scoop du Jour."

"She knows already," he said.

Now, even though I am not one speck anxious for the play to get here, I partly am.

October 30

Since Halloween is on Saturday we had our school parade today, only inside on the stage because it was raining. That was A-OK with Madam and Pop and my mom because they got to sit with the Golds and A-OK with me because then I could inspect costumes one at a time.

Mrs. Timony was a caterpillar in a cocoon until she opened her arms and turned into a Monarch butterfly, which was outstanding to me. Ashley dressed up as Annie, which I would not do if I actually was Annie. Robinson was a soccer player and Hannah was Queen of England. She had a crown and a pocketbook and white gloves and all day we called her Your Majesty and she made the queen wave that is hardly like waving at all.

I thought Jonique and I looked unsurpassable

but Melonhead and Sam surpassed us right by. Sam was a wild scientist and Melonhead was wearing a mountain costume that was higher than his head. Sticking out of the top there was a red fireball that was fake, of course, and Melonhead made the announcement of: "Stay at your own risk. I am one super-active volcano."

Then Sam jumped up on a chair and poured the hugest bottle of clear stuff into Melonhead's volcano top and the red fireball bobbled and then it flew up and green foaming lava erupted all over the stage and globbed down the steps and the whole auditorium went nuts from laughing except for Mrs. Washburn who kept telling kids to stop scooping up lava and throwing it.

"Amazing," Pop said. "I've never known anyone to find a better use for an old toilet float ball."

Later we asked Melonhead for the secret of the lava and he said, "Kool-Aid and vinegar and baking soda. I told you you'd be amazed."

"Are we ever," I told him.

Then he took off his mountain which was totally wet and gross and Jonique and I got to see

how it worked and I said, "We should start calling you Buckethead."

He said the only hard part was unsticking the duct tape from his hair and his face.

October 31

Mrs. McBee and Jonique and I brought Halloween cupcakes to the Capitol Hill Retirement Home. They looked like vampires. I mean the cupcakes, not the retired. Mrs. McBee had made fangs out of candy corn and eyes out of mini M&M's. Jonique and I gave the best vampire to our friend, Mrs. Flora Hennessy, who we know from Bingo and who loves to hear me sing my heart out. When she saw us she said, "Do I know you?"

I said, "Of course you do! It's Jonique and Lucy Rose!"

"We are in disguise," Jonique said.

"You're a horse," Mrs. Hennessy said.

"I'm the horse," Jonique said. "Lucy Rose is the bareback rider."

"Mrs. McBee made our costume, even my tutu and my fake legs," I said. "My real ones are in the back horse legs."

"You have a tutu," Mrs. Hennessy said again.

"Yes," I said.

"You have fake legs," she said.

"Do you want me to sing you a song?" I asked her.

"Yes," she said.

So I sang "Tomorrow" because that's the 1st song that came in my head and Mrs. Hennessy held on to my hand and smiled a gigantic smile and patted Jonique on her horse head.

"I know who you are!" she said.

"Of course you do," I told her.

"You're a singing horse," she said.

At night my mom took Sam and Melonhead and Hannah and Jonique and me trick-or-treating, and even after I threw away all my licorice Jonique and I still had 3 or more pounds of candy. The biggest attraction was the McBees' cemetery but one of the admiring people was Mrs. Small who I happen to know sells houses for her job. She and the McBees were talking their heads off. I say P-U times 2.

NOVEMBER

November 1

These days when the phone rings, I pick up fast. Tonight it was a man who asked for Lily so I made my voice sound like I was a secretary and I said, "Who is this calling her, please?"

"Tim Welsh," he said.

"Mr. Welsh?" I asked him.

"Yes," he said.

"It's Lucy Rose," I said. "Sorry for sounding so grown-up."

My mom talked to him for about a century and when she hung up she said, "I'm the set designer for *Annie*."

"Congratulations!" I said and gave her a great hug.

November 2

On our walk to school I said, "Jonique, guess what? MY MOM got a promotion to be the *Annie* set designer."

"Guess what else?" she said. "MY mom gets to

sew costumes for Annie and 21 orphans and Daddy Warbucks and Miss Hannigan and Sandy the dog."

"Wow!" I said. "I can't believe that out of all the parents our moms are the lucky ducks that got picked."

We were so excited that we ate Jonique's Pringles from her lunch.

November 3

Today was the 1st rehearsal. Here's what gave me irritation: Ashley kept singing "Tomorrow" and wearing her wig. Plus she said from now on everybody has to call her Annie. And her mom made a movie of every single thing she did.

What made me un-irritated was learning the Hard-Knock dance. Mrs. Cunningham said I'm a natural.

November 4

I called Jonique and told what I read when I was eyedropping in my mom's calendar book: "Dinner at Ned's."

"I hope he's a terrible cook," Jonique said.

"Nobody would want a boyfriend that makes bad food."

"I hope he makes beets," I said. "She can't stand the smell of them."

November 5

Today we acted. Kathleen and Robinson practiced being French maids in the hall with a 3rd grade mom who is named Babette and comes from France and lived in a city called Nice that is nice but you pronounce it like the niece that is the opposite of nephew. I am pretty good at French speaking on account of knowing a la mode and bon voyage and Scoop du Jour and ooh la la, but nice Nice is confusing to me.

Since Mr. Welsh is the director he gave the directions. He told Ashley: "Look sweet and stand up straight. You are a charming orphan and you need to make the audience love you and have sympathy for your hard-knock life." And he told me: "Miss Hannigan, you should look grumpy, hunched over and unsteady on your feet. You are a mean woman who drinks too much and takes advantage of parentless children. You need to hide your charms so the audience will not like you."

Afterwards I told him, "Mr. Welsh, I don't want the audience not to like me. Can't Miss Hannigan be good?"

"If they like you, the play will fall apart. No one will feel like Annie needs to be rescued from a nice person," Mr. Welsh said. "Miss Hannigan has to be played by a great actress, someone who can give her a personality. That's why I chose you."

"That's a pleasing thing to hear but I still would rather be Annie," I said.

"Have fun with it, Lucy Rose," he said. "Become Miss Hannigan. But not in the classroom, of course."

"I'll try," I said.

"Break a leg, Lucy Rose," he told me.

That is theater language for: "Do a good job."

He did not say break a leg to Melonhead and Sam. He said, "Stop kung fu fighting in the aisle."

November 6

My mom and I ate our egg sandwiches on the walk to school so she could show her stage drawings to

Mr. Welsh and when he saw them all he could say was "Wowie-pizzowie!"

I squeezed my mom's hand so she would know that I was proud in the extreme.

"I have to share the credit," she said. "My friend Ned is a professional set builder. He gave me great advice."

"I have to go," I said and I ran to my classroom.

After school, Madam and Pop and my mom came to play rehearsal. Mrs. Mannix came by herself because Harry is an orphan and also to help my mom draw the orphanage on the giant cloth that came in the mail from Setting the Scene catalog. Also no one could believe that Mrs. McBee made every orphan a costume. They're like giant pillowcases with head holes and arm holes. Ashley said, "What are they supposed to be?"

That made me so mad I said, "Haven't you ever seen orphan clothes before?"

The truth is I don't actually know what those costumes are supposed to be but I'm sure they will be great because Mrs. McBee is the absolute Queen of Crafts.

Then Mrs. McBee said, "Look what I found at

Goodwill!" She held up 2 clompy black boots that are entirely scruffy and all I could think was "That's not what I call a good find."

Then she said, "They're perfect for you, Miss Hannigan!"

So I said, "Thank you," even though I didn't feel thankful. What I felt was ugly.

November 7

Mr. McBee painted their fence that, if you ask me, already looked fine. This fixing-up jag is worrying my head right off. It could be normal because the McBees are one family that loves a project. Or it could be terrible. When Mrs. Greeley wanted to sell her house, her nephew fixed the yard so it would look like it was inviting to buyers and it must have because now the Proskys live in it. The house, not the yard. I know Jonique doesn't know she's moving because if she did she'd tell me on account of we don't keep secrets. Except I'm keeping this one.

Tonight Madam had to give a speech in Arlington, Virginia, called Happy Siblings. Siblings is my Word of the Day. It means brothers and sisters and I agree that they should be happy.

Since Pop went with Madam for company, I had a babysitter named Phoebe Lewis, who is in 9th and has hair that's divine and is going to get her driving license when she's 16 and she already can't wait. She made me a root beer float and we played Chinese checkers and I won.

This would have been a dream night for me but it wasn't because my mom was having dinner with Ned Eastman. When she came home at 10:30 AT NIGHT, I was still secretly awake and I heard her tell Phoebe that she had a great time.

November 9

P-U. That Ned does nothing but call us. Here is what I heard him say before my mom yelled for me and I had to hang up but quick: "I'll bring you all the flowers you want."

I will tell you one thing: I don't want any.

November 10

Today the orphans took up the whole stage so there was no room for my mom to paint and no kids for Mrs. McBee to measure, so they sat on folding chairs and talked their heads off. I listened my head off.

My mom said, "Tell me how it's going."

"I'm glad I have costumes to sew or I'd do nothing but worry about how to come up with the money," Mrs. McBee said.

"You will," my mom told her.

"I hope," Mrs. McBee said. "It's a fortune."

The only thing I know that costs a fortune is a house.

November 11

Sam's mom came to rehearsal to bring us fruit for energy and his dad came to take pictures of us practicing. He took a lot of me, so I felt like I was the star. Also he took one of me with Clayton Briggs who plays Miss Hannigan's no-good brother named Rooster. Just like me, in real life he is nice.

Mrs. Mannix was Mrs. McBee's assistant and they were talking even though Mrs. Mannix had a whole line of pins sticking out of her mouth which I was going to tell her is unsafe in the extreme. But before I could, Mrs. Mannix said, "I've been meaning to thank you for the cookies, Lola. They were great."

Mrs. McBee spit out the pins. "I was glad to get them out of my house and into yours," Mrs. McBee said. "Now tell me how you're feeling."

"Tired but good," Mrs. Mannix said. "People seem to think I'm on my last leg, though. Nell Conroy dropped off soup. Eddie at Grubb's said if I was overwhelmed he'd drop off Harry's cough syrup. And every M.O.T.H. seems to know I'm having a baby. I had planned on keeping our happy news quiet until Dan got back but my own mother-in-law heard about it on the playground. I have no idea how word got out."

Mrs. McBee looked quizzy at me and said, "I wonder."

I didn't wonder at all.

November 12

This is a sad, mad, bad, unglad day. Mrs. McBee brought my costume to school and when I saw it, all I felt like doing was crying. Even worse, Ashley's red dress is a beaut and her party dress is so deluxe that when Mrs. Timony saw it she clapped and Ashley's mom kept saying, "Twirl for the camera, Doll."

My costume is so ugly that when I tried it on everybody laughed, especially Ashley. To go with my clompy boots, I have falling-down socks and a baggy dress with brown polka dots on it and a raggedy apron and hair curlers made of pink sponges.

Then Ashley's mom asked Mrs. McBee, "Would you mind if I add a few sequins to Doll's party dress?"

That made me burning mad and when Mrs. McBee said, "Sure," I felt like my head could explode from being frustrated.

Then Mr. Welsh did explode at Melonhead and Sam because instead of practicing being dog-catchers they were jumping around with pencils poking out of their ears and nostrils, which I have to say was hilarious in the extreme, but Mrs. Cunningham said, "Adam and Sam! Remove those immediately! Professional actors absolutely never put pencils in their noses or ears."

"I know that's right," Jonique said.

"Unless it's in the script, but I never heard of a script like that," I said.

Jonique was wearing her Sandy suit and looking as cute as a real dog with tannish fur and a black nose and a tail that moves when she crawls. She already knows her line. It is "Arf!"

We almost had a disaster because the stage curtain was drooping like it was going to fall down but Mr. Alswang and Hannah's dad rescued it which was a ton of work because even though it's made of nothing but cloth, it's heavy.

Ashley's mom did not help. I think she was tired from sewing 983 or more sequins on Annie's party dress. Plus Ashley got shining shoes that are a little bit high heel that she wore all day so everybody would praise her to pieces. Marisol kept saying she had the best costume in the show.

"Isn't my dress beautiful?" Ashley asked me.

Madam says that people who are not raised in barns know that sometimes you have to say something nice even when you do not feel like it. So I said, "It's pretty."

"Is that all you have to say?" Ashley said.

"Yes," I told her.

She stomped her party shoes across the stage.

November 14

Pop and I were eating clementines and spitting the seeds off the porch in case they might grow and that's when he said, "What's the Scoop du Jour?"

I told about my terrible costume and Ashley's great costumes and how she keeps telling me she got to be Annie because she's the greatest singer. "Plus her mom told Mr. Welsh that Ashley needs a clip-on microphone so her singing will go to the back of the room," I said.

"Hmm," Pop said. "What is the worst problem?"

"Not being Annie," I said.

"Are you kidding?" Pop said. "I say, thank goodness you aren't Annie! Anyone can be Annie. But Miss Hannigan is funny, Lucy Rose. Not everybody can play funny."

"Can I?" I asked him.

"Can you?" Pop said. "Lucy Rose, you were born funny and I think you were born to play Miss Hannigan."

I liked that talk of ours.

I am what Madam calls IN A STATE. Not like Texas. I am in the state of anxiety. Today at Stanton Park when Jonique was throwing a tennis ball to Gumbo and I was eavesdropping, I heard Mrs. McBee confessing to my mom: "Lily, I'm up nights worrying. The truth is I'm gambling with our family savings."

Then my mom said, "I have no worries, Lola. I think it's a sure thing."

That is the worst advice I have ever heard in my life. If my mom was Dear Lucy Rose, I think she would be fired.

I can't figure out if the McBees are moving or if they are broke from Mrs. McBee's gambling. Maybe they have to move on account of her gambling.

Tonight I asked my mom, "How much money do we have?"

She asked me, "Are you afraid we don't have enough?"

"I'm just wondering," I said.

"We have enough and a little more," she said. "Daddy helps pay for things you need and I make enough to pay for our house and the electric bill, the phone, groceries, and some extras like movie tickets and yellow mums. Every payday, I put money in a savings account in case we have an emergency. And when we want something big, like a sofa, I work overtime."

"You do a good job," I told her.

Yesterday after dinner, I figured out a funny way to make Miss Hannigan walk so her boots flop around. My mom helped me learn my lines by doing all the other parts. Tonight I am exhausted in the extreme because we had late rehearsal that lasted until

9 PM at night because Mrs. Cunningham said our dancing is a long way from good. We had to order pizza by delivery so we wouldn't perish to death. Melonhead ate 6 pieces plus my pepperoni and Sam's crusts.

I danced until my legs were beat tired but the greatest thing was when Mrs. Cunningham told me, "Lucy Rose, you're getting better with every step."

"I'm breaking both my legs," I said.

Then Mr. Welsh said, "Adam and Sam, the dog-catching nets are not swords. And Ashley, let's hear you sing 'Tomorrow.'"

When she was done I remembered what Mr. Welsh said about being on the acting team so I hollered, "Great job!"

Next Mr. Welsh said, "Lucy Rose, sing your solo."

Then, right in front of the whole complete cast, Ashley hissed, "So low we can't hear you."

I feel fed up with that girl.

November 19

We had no rehearsal because Mr. Welsh has to get a canal on the roots of his teeth, which is something I don't know why anybody would want. Instead we went to Jonique's and Mrs. McBee gave us buttermilk biscuits with the kind of honey that comes in a plastic bear. "This house is a snack palace," I said.

"Come anytime," Mrs. McBee said.

So I said, "Thank you, my queen."

Then I did discreet searching around the house to see if it looked like they were out of money.

It didn't.

November 20

When I got to my grandparents' after school, Madam inspected me and said, "Lucy Rose, you need some downtime."

That is the same as relaxing. Then Madam had the idea of making the biggest exception in her life about TV on school nights and we sat on the sofa and ate stir-fry stringbeans and watched the olden days show of *Bewitched*. I felt nothing but relaxed.

Also, I got a card from my aunt Marguerite that lives in Japan and it said, "Good luck on opening night!" and it came with 2 things I collect. 1. A stamp. 2. The palindrome of BIRD RIB, which is one of the best I ever heard. I e-mailed it to my dad straight away.

November 21

I heard my mom saying to Madam, "Don't tell Lucy Rose."

I think you should be allowed to eavesdrop if you're the one they're talking about.

November 22

My book report is due tomorrow. My book, that used to be my mom's when she was 9, is about *The Secret of the Hidden Staircase*. It is a mystery starring Nancy Drew who is a teenager and a detective that has her own car. There is only one part I do not like about that book. Nancy Drew has a boyfriend and his name is: Ned.

November 23

All morning I was waiting for the intercom to say, "Lucy Rose Reilly, please report to the principal's office," and when it did, I reported so fast that Madam hadn't even finished signing me out 4 hours early. We jumped in the car and Pop zoomed us over the bridge and past the Pentagon and to the Reagan National Airport. We parked in number D13, which Pop said we had to remember if we ever wanted to see the purple station wagon again.

The arrivals TV said my dad's plane was coming to gate C27, which was another number we had to remember if we ever wanted to find him, which we did.

When we got to the waiting spot I stood right in the middle. I was wearing my pink Glamma skirt and a green sweater with fringes on the sleeve end-ings that was a present from Aunt Pansy because she got it on sale. Also I had on orange tights and my red cowgirl boots and my yellow bandana. I picked these clothes because I think people notice a person who is colorful and I wanted my dad to notice me first thing.

When the plane let out, I saw 2 sunflowers sticking up over all the heads of the arriving and I knew my dad was holding them. But then I saw he was only holding one because Glamma had the other one. I ran so fast that I fell over a suitcase that belonged to a man who wasn't the nicest and I hollered, "I'm sorry!" and kept going and when I got close, I threw myself and landed in both of their arms and nearly knocked Glamma off her high heels and she started barking like crazy. Then I figured out it wasn't Glamma barking. It was her purse. Inside there was a dog that was as puny as Jake, the 3rd grade guinea pig. The dog has the name of Darling Girl and the same color hair as Glamma and according to Shiralee that is called Frivolous Fawn.

"Look at you," my dad said. "You're even prettier."

"I like your lip naked," I told him.

Glamma said she did too on account of she's against mustaches. I take her hair ideas seriously because she has a haircutting license that came from the government.

On the drive to the hotel, I sat in the back with Glamma and my dad, and Darling Girl sat up front on Madam's lap. Pop drove the long way so Glamma could see the Washington Monument, which looks just like a giant pencil, only white.

At the hotel, I jumped out and ran straight to Check In and said, "Hello there, Mr. Smiley!" which is his actual name.

He said, "Hello, Lucy Rose!"

So I said, "How's your daughter that lives on a mountain in Vermont and makes necklaces for money?"

He said she's coming home when it's Christmas and he's cooking a ham. "He knows us," I told Glamma. "We always stay here when Dad visits and once Mr. Smiley gave me a free comb from behind the desk."

This trip, my dad got a 1-person room that's named 705 and Glamma and I got Room 711 with 2 double beds and 2 sinks so we can brush our teeth at the exact same time.

In Room 711, I danced on my bed with Darling Girl while Glamma made her hair taller and changed out of her traveling high heels that are color of green Sweet Tarts into her walking high heels that are black with cherries swinging on the toes. Madam is not the kind that wears jeans in front of the public but Glamma is. Also her nails are covered with red polish.

"You're a beaut," I told her.

"You are too," she said and sprayed me with perfume called Parisian Night that smells very ooh-la-la. Then we put Darling Girl into her pink dog purse and rode the elevator to the lobby so my dad could walk us to the Natural History Museum.

When we got there, we went in the lobby and Glamma said, "Amazing," about a stuffed elephant that used to be real.

And my dad said, "You're my best girls," about us and took our picture in front of the elephant.

And then the guard came running over and said, "Hey, you there! Dogs aren't allowed here!"

So I said, "Even when they are in a dog purse and not one speck of bother?"

And he said, "Yes, even then."

"That's okay," I told him. "Because I'm starving to absolute perishable pieces."

At the tourist truck in front of the museum I got a chili dog and Glamma bought Shiralee a shirt that says F.B.I. Agent, which I don't think anybody will believe, and she told the man I'd have a Coke but my dad said I would have a ginger ale because my mom is against me having caffeine. I didn't say it but it felt a little good that he still knows my rules.

We had to take a taxi back on account of Glamma had 3 blisters on her feet and my legs felt like they were exhausted.

November 23—Only at night.
2 hours past my bedtime

After dinner, my mom met us at the ice cream store. She and Glamma hugged and my mom said, "Hi, Bob."

Then my dad said, "It's good to see you, Lily."

So she said, "You too."

Then he said, "Ladies, may I take your orders?" like he was our waiter and that made me crack up.

My dad and my mom and I all got the same, which was peppermint except mine had sprinkles. Glamma got coffee for herself and vanilla for Darling Girl. Then we had a visit. That is one activity that I love.

Back in our hotel, Glamma and I got washed and brushed and she said I could keep the tiny shampoos because she gets hers for free from the Beauty Spot. Then she tucked me and Darling Girl in my bed and put herself in her bed, and we talked our lips off in the dark. I don't know why but I told about how I eavesdropped and how I'm feeling stress, especially about Ned.

"Who's Ned?" she said.

"A man who wants to have a date with my mom," I said.

"Your mom's a sweetie," she said.

"That doesn't mean she should have a date," I said.

Then I thought of something awful in the extreme. "Has my dad had a date in Ann Arbor?" I asked her.

"No," Glamma said. "But I imagine one day he will."

"P-U on that," I said.

"I know it's hard for you," she said.

"Very hard," I said, and I had to confide another thing. "The McBees are moving and Mrs. McBee is a gambler."

"I'm so sorry to hear that because I know Jonique is important to you," Glam said. "What does your mom say?"

"Nothing," I said, "I'm not telling her I know because I wasn't supposed to be listening on account of some things are private and that's called having respect and I don't want to make her feel like she's disappointed."

"How about Madam?" Glamma asked.

"Same problem. Lately I've been rule stretching like mad," I said.

"Are you sorry?" Glamma asked.

"No. If I didn't listen I would never know the news," I said. "Plus I was compelled."

"You were compelled?" she said.

"Yes. That's my Word of the Day. It's when you can't stop yourself," I said.

"I've been compelled before myself," she said.

"I'm glad I told you," I said.

"Me too," Glamma said. "And you know you can always call me long distance."

"You know, I used to think long distance was the same as discreetly," I said and we had a big laugh about that.

Then I said, "Do you know what I should do?"

"Let me sleep on it," Glamma said.

She is sleeping on it right now. I'm not on account of my brain's dancing around thinking about doing the play tomorrow.

November 24—Day of the Play! at the crack of 7 AM

This morning while we were brushing Darling Girl's teeth, I asked Glamma, "Did you sleep on my problems?"

"Yep," she said. "And I thought that since we're meeting your dad in the hotel restaurant in 3 minutes, you might want to put your troubles on the table and get his ideas too."

"A-OK with me," I said. "But I am not telling about Ned."

After I ate my chocolate pancake with strawberry syrup, I did tell the other things. "It's a bad feeling to be worrying about everybody plus this eavesdropping is making me feel like I am guilty," I said.

Then my dad said, "When you eavesdrop on the bus like Pop does, and the person gets off before you know the end of their story, you can make it up. Your ending might be better or worse than what really happened and that's fine because you're a writer and writers can write fiction. But when you eavesdrop on people you love you worry because you can't choose how their story ends."

"That's it exactly," I said. "And if I ask them, I have to confess about being a spy."

"Nobody likes confessing," my dad said. "But people who love you forgive you."

"I myself have been forgiven for worse things," Glam said.

"Me too," my dad said.

"What on earth did you people do?" I asked.

They did not answer that question.

"Everyone makes mistakes," my dad said. "Smart people say they're sorry."

"If they have maturity, which I do," I said.

"Yards of it," my dad said.

The same exact day only after school

Jonique and I were walking past Grubb's on our way home and feeling too excited to stand it. That's when I had my sharpest idea. I told Jonique and she gave me a quarter and I had a dime and a ton of pennies and even though I was short of a nickel Eddie said I could pay it later.

Now I'm home, eating celery with peanut butter and raisins because my mom says actors need protein.

When I'm done I'm putting on my costume and going to opening night.

10:30 PM at night. if you can believe it!

This night was nothing but fabulinity plus the best one of my life and anybody that had this night would have self-esteem galore and, boy, do I ever.

I feel like I want to tell the last things first but that is confusing so I'm starting at when I got to the auditorium and saw the stage, which caused me to shout, "My mom is a genius!" at the tip-top of my lungs.

Then Hannah and I showed my dad and Glamma the backstage and I told them, "Mom and her helpers painted the orphanage building and put up those fake trees so people will think we are actually outside, plus for the inside she built orphan beds and for Daddy Warbucks' house she made those silver vases of red roses and that golden statue. That's to show that he's as rich as anything. Clayton's mom helped make that desk that looks like real wood but is actually painted cardboard. And Mom got that olden days telephone, which is a clue to the audience that they are going back in time because that's when *Annie* is supposed to be happening."

My dad told my mom, "Lily, you did a terrific job."

Glamma said it was "FAN-tastic!" She always says the fan part louder and longer than the tastic so we will know she really thinks it and isn't just being polite.

"Thank you," my mom said. "I had a lot of help."

"Let's get moving," I said because I did not want my dad to hear the word Ned.

By 7:30 PM, the auditorium was popping full and the lights went out and Mrs. Timony started up with the piano and the curtain opened and there were the orphans, fake sleeping in their fake beds. Then Annie tries to make an escape, only Miss Hannigan catches her and just this afternoon when I was with Jonique I figured out how to give her some more personality.

I wandered across the stage with my droopiest shoulders, wearing my baggy dress and my clomping

boots with my falling-down socks and curlers in my hair. Plus I was carrying a cup. When I got to the middle, I looked right at the audience and wobbled and then, when they were looking right at me, I smiled. Everybody cracked up like you couldn't believe. That's because before it was showtime, I chewed up the Black Jack gum I got when we stopped at Grubb's this afternoon and stuck it on 3 of my top front teeth. And I have to say this: When I'm Mrs. Hannigan, I am a laugh riot.

I'm also snappy mean. When I was yelling at the orphans, I made myself act so screechy and stompy that if I was an orphan, my nerves would shake.

For the whole, entire show I felt like I was shining, like I was the ultra-best Miss Hannigan there ever was. That is not a brag because it's the truth. Every time I finished acting people clapped like crazy and I heard Pop snorting, because when he thinks something is hilarious, he laughs so hard that air gets stuck inside his nose. Here's what I decided: Even though Annie has the good clothes, Miss Hannigan is the part for me. The only bad thing was that the play zipped by and when it was over I wished it wasn't because I felt like a dream of mine had come true. When I made my bow, the room went wild with applauding. I did Hannah's queen wave at them. Ashley bowed last because she's the star. Everybody cheered for her too and I could hear her mom yelling, "That's my Doll!"

Right at that absolute instant, I thought Mr. Welsh was right. When you're a great actress, you want EVERYBODY to be great too because that's the way the play will be the greatest. When the lights came on, my dad and Glamma gave me 1 dozen pink roses, which is something I thought you had to be at least a teenager to get. My mom and Madam and Pop gave me and Jonique daisies that are called Marguerites. Mrs. McBee gave me the hug of my life and I gave it back to her. Melonhead told me I was funny which made me feel delightful and made Pop say I was basking in glory which means lolling in it, which was true because it felt just like I was famous.

Then Pop said, "Jonique, you were a fine dog. Adam and Sam, you were such great dogcatchers, I feared for Jonique. And Hannah, you were a perfect orphan."

"Plus," I said, "she was a big help with Harry who was not perfect at all."

Then my mom grabbed my hand and said,

"Come with me, Lucy Rose, I want you to meet Ned Eastman."

That made me think I would throw up on Miss Hannigan's boots but I didn't because my mom was pulling me and she didn't slow down until we practically crashed into an old man who said, "Hello," to us.

So my mom said, "This is Lucy Rose."

"Hi," I said and scrunched myself down in case Ned was on the lookout for us.

"You're a fine actress," the man said. "I'm Ned Eastman."

"But you're old!" I shouted because I was feeling nothing but shock.

I could tell my mom was feeling like she was mortified.

"I am old," he said. "I'm 69. This is my wife, Mary Louise. She's a babe of 64."

"Oh," I said because I could not even think.

"And this is our granddaughter, Olivia," he said.

Then Mrs. Eastman said: "Lucy Rose, your mom told us all about you when she came to our house for dinner. I'm so glad we got to see the play. When you're a big star on Broadway, I'm going to tell everyone that I know you personally."

That made me feel flattered to bits.

Then Ned said, "Lily, the sets are first-rate."

"I couldn't have done it without your help," my mom said.

Then my dad came up and I said, "Hey, Dad! Look! THIS is Ned Eastman. Plus his WIFE and Olivia."

"Ned is the chief set builder at Channel 6," my mom told my dad. "He and I have been working together since September, redesigning the set for *Good Day Washington*. Finally, after lots of meetings, lots of hours and pots of coffee, it's finished and beautiful."

"It was my last project before I retire," Ned told my dad.

"No," my mom said. "Your last project was finding silk roses, an old phone, and all the other props we needed for *Annie*."

I threw my arms around Ned Eastman's middle and gave him a squeezing hug and said, "THANK YOU, MY FRIEND!"

I invited the Eastmans to the cast party that was in the main hall by the nurse's office and Olivia begged so they did even though she's only 5. I think they were glad because the Kempners brought cookies that were assorted and Mrs. Melon brought Nilla Wafers, which are her favorite because they don't stain. Max Lewis who was Daddy Warbucks passed out sugar cookies. The best dessert of all was lemon bars, made by Mrs. McBee.

Jonique and I brought some of the assorted to our retired friends that took up all of Row 2 during the play. Mrs. Zuckerman said she loved the show and Mr. Emanuel Woods gave us 2 peppermints each but Mrs. Hennessy stared at us, even though Jonique said, "It's nice to see you, Mrs. Hennessy."

When she didn't say anything back, I smoothed my Miss Hannigan makeup off my face with my hands and I said, "Mrs. Hennessy, do you recognize me now?"

"Of course I do," she said.

"I knew you would," I told her.

"You used to be a horse," she said.

I didn't know what to say about that so I just said, "I feel like I'm lucky to see you," and I gave her one of my mints and went back to the auditorium to look for my mom who wasn't there.

Who WAS there was a man and a lady and

Ashley. She was holding the biggest pile of flowers ever made and the man was taking her picture and saying, "You were the best!"

The lady said, "I was really impressed."

Then the man saw me and said, "You were very good too."

"Thank you," I told him.

"I'm Ashley's dad," he said. "This is my girl-friend, Jen."

Jen said, "Glad to meet you. The show was very unique."

"You can't be very unique," Ashley said. "Just unique or not unique."

"Really?" Jen said.

"Ask Lucy Rose if you don't believe me," Ashley said.

I gave Ashley a smile that I really meant because even though she had been nothing but dreadful for weeks, right at that minute I felt sympathy. Then I said, "You were a really good Annie, Ashley. Better than I would have been."

"Thanks," she said. "You were a really good old hag."

That's when I heard my mom calling for cleanup

helpers, so I ran back and helped her pick up old paper cups and put them in the trash can and that's when I told her, "Of all the nights in my life this one was the absolute greatest and to tell you the truth, I feel like my heart is flying from happiness."

"I feel like my heart is flying too," my mom said.

"How come?" I asked her.

"Because when your heart flies, so does mine," she said.

"Automatically?" I asked.

"Automatically," she said.

Right then Mr. Jenkins, who is the custodian, flipped the light switch up and down and said, "I hate to chase out my good helpers but the rules are that everyone has to be out by 10 o'clock."

"Right-O," I said and I was a little glad because after the most exciting night like this one was, used paper cup hunting is a little bit on the boring side of things.

We walked home from the play in a clump. Jonique was in front, with Glamma and Darling Girl, who was wearing her fake ruby-covered collar. Darling Girl, not Glam. She was wearing her black jeans that are called sassy and a sweater with glitter on it and has more style than anybody could dream up. Jonique was happy in the extreme on account of she got to carry the dog purse.

My dad was walking with Harry who was acting completely uncontrollable. Mr. McBee and my mom were in a clump with Madam and Pop who were holding hands, which I wish they wouldn't because Ashley tells everybody they are too old to be doing that. Mr. McBee was telling about zoning. I don't know what that is but I do know it's tedious in the extreme, so I didn't eavesdrop for a 2nd second on them.

I walked by myself, which I didn't mind because I wanted privacy so I could think about all the times people clapped for my acting and also about being on Broadway, which probably won't happen until I am 20 years old and move to New York.

Mrs. Mannix and Mrs. McBee were the last ones because Mrs. Mannix is a slow walker on account of that baby is weighing her down.

Then, right when my mind was lolling in happiness I heard something out of the corner of my ear and it was Mrs. McBee saying, "I'll bet my bottom dollar you're going to have a girl."

My stomach felt like it fell on the sidewalk because I know about bottom dollars from singing "Tomorrow." They are the very last dollar a person has. I spun around and even though I didn't plan it at all, my arm flew up like a policeman saying, "Stop," and I said, "Mrs. McBee, I have to talk to you in private. RIGHT NOW."

Mrs. Mannix gave me a little smile and scooted up to be with Harry. My heart was beating so hard I felt it on my ribs and I felt scared inside and I grabbed onto Mrs. McBee's hand and I said, "Mrs. McBee, I am BEGGING you: Please, STOP GAMBLING!"

"What?" she said.

"Mrs. McBee," I said. "You have to TRY. THINK of your FAMILY! Think of your BOTTOM DOLLARS! STOP before you GAMBLE your LIFE SAVINGS away and GO BROKE and have to MOVE to NORTH CAROLINA. Think of ME. You McBees are my BEST friends and I am feeling like I'm HEARTBROKEN inside. Plus devastated."

"We love Capitol Hill," she said. "We're not moving."

"But you miss your sister," I said.

"That's true," Mrs. McBee said.

I let out my breath. "You are my queen," I told her.

"I may be a queen but I am NOT a gambler," she said. "I don't know what put that idea in your head, child, but if my pastor heard, he'd give me a talking-to that would never end."

"But I HEARD you tell my mom you were gambling with your savings and that you had to come up with money," I said. "And I heard Mr. McBee say he's trying to afford it. And I just one second ago heard you bet Mrs. Mannix your absolute bottom dollar."

Mrs. McBee had the look of being baffled. Then she smiled right at me. "Lucy Rose, your mom mentioned that you've become something of an eavesdropper," she said.

"And eyedropper," I said. "I'm sorry about not having respect but, BELIEVE ME, it's a LUCKY thing I did listen. What if I didn't and NOBODY stopped you and you LOST all your money?"

"I think you'd be less worried if you had eavesdropped more," she said. "But I'm glad you didn't because as much as I adore you, I don't think you need to know all about my bank account. And don't worry, our money is in a good place."

I felt like I could drop over from relief. "I'm sorry I spied," I said.

"And I'm grateful that you care so much about us," Mrs. McBee said. "It takes courage to tell your friends when you think they are doing the wrong thing."

"I was afraid I didn't have courage because I kept thinking, what if you got hopping mad at me?" I told her. "That would be horrible because I'm not kidding when I call you my queen."

"You are my little nut," she said. "My precious little nut."

"Thank you," I said.

We walked without talking for a few minutes and then she said, "Lucy Rose, this isn't like Mrs. Mannix and the baby, is it? You haven't told the neighborhood I have a gambling problem, have you?

"I would NEVER," I said. "I didn't even tell Jonique."

I felt so full of happiness and relief that my arms shivered, which made me glad I was wearing the

Annie T-shirt my dad bought me from the money-collecting committee because they need to pay for next year's play, which I hope is *The Sound of Music,* because I would like to be 16 going on 17 or else that nun that plays the guitar.

Later, when we were back in Room 711 and ready for bed, I couldn't stop thinking about the greatness of this night and how all my problems disappeared and even though I didn't tell Glam, I'm pretty sure she knew what I was thinking because right before she fell asleep she said: "So, how about that Ned Eastman, Lucy Rose?"

"How about him?" I said and laughed so hard that Darling Girl yipped at me.

November 25

I got our wake-up call ultra-early this morning because after all that acting last night, I knew I would be starving for breakfast buffet. Plus Glamma needs time to put on her face, which is makeup, and, by the way, her eyelashes come in a box and get stuck on with glue and according to her, movie stars wear them all the time. I watched her close-up so I can learn how to glue because I figured out that Broadway stars need to know that in case they ever have to be in a movie.

At 8 AM Glam and my dad and I walked to school. We picked up Jonique on the way and I gave her a blueberry muffin that was left over from my buffet. Since we got to school a little early they stood around on the playground and talked to other people's parents and, for politeness, I hung around them. That's when Ashley came rushing up and my dad said, "Good morning! You were a great Annie last night!"

Instead of thank you she said, "Are you Lucy Rose's dad?"

"I am that lucky man," my dad said.

"Are you a millionaire?" she asked him.

My dad made the biggest laugh. "No," he said. "I'm a teacher. I'm rich in good times."

"So YOU do NOT have a MILLION dollars?" she asked him, which was rude because, according to Madam, you are not supposed to ask people how much money they have even if you are so curious you can't stand it.

"That's correct," my dad said. "I do not."

"I DIDN'T think so," Ashley said.

Then she put her hands on her hips and stamped her party shoes and said, "YOUR DAUGHTER IS A BIG LIAR."

That made lots of people look at me, including parents and Mr. Jenkins, the custodian.

"I am NOT a liar," I told her. "I NEVER told you my dad was rich."

"You said he was loaded and don't deny it because I heard you at P.E. telling Jonique, 'My dad has a million,' " she said.

"I never said dollars," I told her. "And, BY THE WAY, you should NOT have been EAVESDROP-PING on my PRIVATE conversation because you should have RESPECT."

"If it's not dollars, what do you have a million of?" Ashley asked my dad and her voice was crabby in the extreme and every single body heard it.

"Well, I have a million happy memories," he said. "A million dreams for my students. A million hugs for my daughter. And I feel like I have a mil-lion chores to do."

But she was stomping off, singing a song about my pants being on fire, going straight to Room 7 to tell everybody I'm a liar. Luckily, Melonhead and

Sam and Hannah and Clayton and Kathleen told her I wasn't. Then Ashley hollered, "Marisol, tell them Lucy Rose is a liar."

At first Marisol didn't say anything. At second she looked like she was feeling scared. Then she said, "You are my best friend, Ashley, but I think Lucy Rose is not a liar."

"She is too," Ashley said.

"Remember how you told me that you weren't going to try out for Annie and then you did?" Marisol said.

"That wasn't a lie," Ashley told her. "That was a misunderstanding."

"Well," Marisol said, "I think you were misunderstanding when you heard Lucy Rose talking about millions."

That made Ashley wild with anger and she flopped down in her chair to ignore us. That turned out to be right when Mrs. Timony came in and found everybody else not behaving.

"Thank you for setting a good example, Ashley," Mrs. Timony said, which made the class feel like they were irritated to pieces, which they still were at recess.

"Aren't you steaming?" Melonhead asked me.

"Not so steaming," I said.

"I am," Sam said. "She only heard a small bit of the story and then she went nuts about what she thought you were talking about only she was 100 percent wrong."

"That could happen to anybody," I said.

November 26—Thanksgiving

This morning, my mom and I went to Madam and Pop's to help cook. When we were rolling dough and Madam was making the pie insides by mixing cherries with apricot jam that she made herself in the summer, I said, "Get ready for disappointment."

"Why?" my mom asked.

"Because I didn't listen to Madam's recommendation about privacy. And I broke 1 of Pop's 3 Rules for a Happy Family. Plus I stretched your rule so far I can't believe myself on account of I've been doing nothing but eavesdropping and eyedropping on you and the McBees and Madam and Mrs. Mannix, but she was by accident," I said.

"Really?" my mom said.

"Really," I said. "This is not a thing I would kid about."

Then nobody said anything. "I needed to know what was going on," I said. "But the thing about dropping is that it's hard to stop, even if it gives you misery."

"What did you find out?" Madam asked.

"Information, but it turned out I was wrong about every single thing except for Mrs. Mannix having a baby."

"What were you wrong about?" my mom asked me.

"Ned," I said. "He turned out to not be 1 bit of a dread or one bit of a boyfriend."

"I told you he was just a friend," my mom said.

"When I listened he sounded boyfriendish," I told her.

"I should have done a better job of explaining about Ned," my mom said. "I'm sorry you were worried."

"About a lot of things," I said. "I thought the McBees were moving and that Mrs. McBee was a gambler. That made me have stress and nerves and thank goodness it's not true."

"I can't imagine Lola gambling," Madam said.

"Well, you could if you heard what I heard," I told her. "That's why starting yesterday, I'm giving up eavesdropping except on strangers, even though I never did figure out what you told Madam to keep secret from me."

"I told her that Glamma was coming to surprise you," my mom said.

"I was surprised," I said. "I'm sorry to make you feel like you're disappointed."

"You told the truth," my mom said. "I can't be disappointed."

We had a 3 people hug at that and I said, "So I guess you are appointed."

That was a joke, you know.

Telling made my heart feel better and made my body feel like I had energy galore. My mom and I boiled cranberries until they turned into jelly before our very eyeballs. When Pop came back from buying the flowers, he filled the turkey with corn bread and put it in the oven. I was in charge of the timer. Madam and I cooked Thanksgiving meat loaf for Gumbo and Darling Girl. And all 4 of us made sweet potatoes with marshmallows on top and plain potatoes with butter on top. Pop made himself a beard out of leftover parsley, which made Madam say, "A good-looking man can wear anything." Which I will tell you privately, is not true.

Glam and my dad spent the day in Georgetown, buying chocolate and also kumquats for a present for Madam. Kumquats are my Word of the Day. They're fruit that look like puny eggs that are orange. Even though they smell interesting, I am not a fan of them because 1. You eat the skin and the insides and 2. I don't like the taste of the insides.

By 6 PM at night everybody was in party clothes and I was wearing the poofiest dress that was a hand-me-down from Aunt Betsy's daughter named Darlene, and lacey tights and my cowgirl boots but not my bandana because Madam said it's not the thing to put on at Thanksgiving. Glamma had on black pants that are divine as anything and a golden shirt with a shining pin that's a turkey with jewels for eyes. My dad wore the tie I mailed him for Father's Day. Pop called my mom's black dress swank, which I am pretty sure is a complimenting thing.

Before dinner we had to stand around the morning room so the grown-ups could eat raw oysters, which is a thing I would never do, because oysters are made of slime. Since I was already perishing from hunger, my dad opened the chocolates so I could eat a piece. My mom ate 1 too, which made her say: "These are so rich."

"Very rich," I told her. "They cost $27.73."

I saw the price sticker on the bottom.

At dinnertime I got to light the candles, which is one job I adore to pieces. Since I made the place cards, my mom and my dad were sitting next to each other. Before we drank pumpkin soup, we all held hands and said what we were grateful for and I said, "Everything."

Dinner took more than 1 hour. I ate 3 scoops of stuffing, the same as my dad. Then I said, "I'm stuffed." Get it?

At 9 PM, the door knocked and it was the McBees because they were our dessert guests plus Mrs. McBee said she had an announcement to make.

"Well, as some of you know," she said and looked right at me, "we've been looking at property and worrying about money. Now all that worry and all that money paid off. Leon and I are buying a small building across from the Eastern Market and Frankie is moving to Washington and we're going to turn it into a bakery."

"Lola thinks it's a bit of a gamble," Mr. McBee said. "But the way she bakes, I say it's a winner."

That news had us all jumping and Gumbo tap dancing on her toenails and Darling Girl yipping her dog head off.

"What are you going to call your bakery?" my mom asked.

"Lucy Rose named it," Mrs. McBee said.

"I did?" I said.

"We're calling it the Baking Divas."

"I never named a bakery before," I said.

November 29

Today Madam and I took my dad and Glamma and Darling Girl to the airport. We drove past the Capitol and the back of the White House and the Washington Monument and Glamma said her favorite thing was the Botanic Garden that we went to on Friday and that is absolutely full of flowers. My dad said, "I liked the International Spy Museum we went to yesterday."

I said, "I can still not believe that they have a radio receiver that is disguised as dog poop."

I am not kidding.

At the airport Glamma said, "This was a FANtastic trip."

"I'm one person who agrees with that," I said.

"I loved being with you, Lucy Rose," my dad said. "I'm sure I will never see a better Miss Hannigan and I'm very proud of the way you solved your problems."

"Actually, I feel like my life is perfect right now," I said. "Except for Ashley."

"Of course," my dad said.

"How's Otis?" I asked him.

"About 95 pounds of constant trouble," he said. "But now when he does something awful I just say, 'Sit on a pan, Otis.' "

"That is a very odd thing to say," I told him. "Does it make him shape up?"

"Not a bit," my dad said. "But it's a great palindrome."

"It's better than great," I said. "It's fabulinity."

 The Tables!

1s

1 x 1 = 1

1 x 2 = 2

1 x 3 = 3

1 x 4 = 4

1 x 5 = 5

1 x 6 = 6

1 x 7 = 7

1 x 8 = 8

1 x 9 = 9

1 x 10 = 10

2s

$2 \times 1 = 2$

$2 \times 2 = 4$

$2 \times 3 = 6$

$2 \times 4 = 8$

$2 \times 5 = 10$

$2 \times 6 = 12$

$2 \times 7 = 14$

$2 \times 8 = 16$

$2 \times 9 = 18$

$2 \times 10 = 20$

3s

$3 \times 1 = 3$

$3 \times 2 = 6$

$3 \times 3 = 9$

$3 \times 4 = 12$

$3 \times 5 = 15$

$3 \times 6 = 18$

$3 \times 7 = 21$

$3 \times 8 = 24$

$3 \times 9 = 27$

$3 \times 10 = 30$

4s

$4 \times 1 = 4$

$4 \times 2 = 8$

$4 \times 3 = 12$

$4 \times 4 = 16$

$4 \times 5 = 20$

$4 \times 6 = 24$

$4 \times 7 = 28$

$4 \times 8 = 32$

$4 \times 9 = 36$

$4 \times 10 = 40$

5s

5 x 1 = 5

5 x 2 = 10

5 x 3 = 15

5 x 4 = 20

5 x 5 = 25

5 x 6 = 30

5 x 7 = 35

5 x 8 = 40

5 x 9 = 45

5 x 10 = 50

6s

$6 \times 1 = 6$

$6 \times 2 = 12$

$6 \times 3 = 18$

$6 \times 4 = 24$

$6 \times 5 = 30$

$6 \times 6 = 36$

$6 \times 7 = 42$

$6 \times 8 = 48$

$6 \times 9 = 54$

$6 \times 10 = 60$

7s

7 x 1 = 7

7 x 2 = 14

7 x 3 = 21

7 x 4 = 28

7 x 5 = 35

7 x 6 = 42

7 x 7 = 49

7 x 8 = 56

7 x 9 = 63

7 x 10 = 70

8s

8 x 1 = 8

8 x 2 = 16

8 x 3 = 24

8 x 4 = 32

8 x 5 = 40

8 x 6 = 48

8 x 7 = 56

8 x 8 = 64

8 x 9 = 72

8 x 10 = 80

9s

9 x 1 = 9

9 x 2 = 18

9 x 3 = 27

9 x 4 = 36

9 x 5 = 45

9 x 6 = 54

9 x 7 = 63

9 x 8 = 72

9 x 9 = 81

9 x 10 = 90

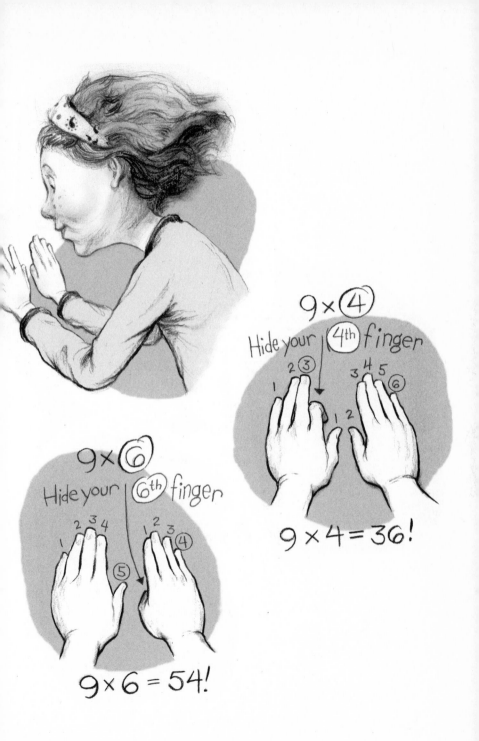

9×4

Hide your 4th finger

$9 \times 4 = 36!$

9×6

Hide your 6th finger

$9 \times 6 = 54!$

10s

10 x 1 = 10

10 x 2 = 20

10 x 3 = 30

10 x 4 = 40

10 x 5 = 50

10 x 6 = 60

10 x 7 = 70

10 x 8 = 80

10 x 9 = 90

10 x 10 = 100

Katy Kelly is just as busy as Lucy Rose. Though she hasn't had a job dancing, singing, or acting, she is a mother of two, a wife of one, and a full-time writer. She lives in Washington, D.C. *Lucy Rose: Busy Like You Can't Believe* is her third book for young readers.